The Filly

The Filly

Mark R. Probst

Cover art and design by Jeffrey Albaugh

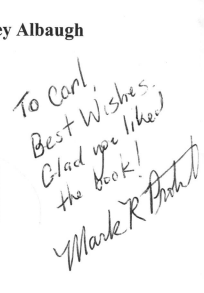

LethePressBooks.com

To Carl,
Best Wishes.
Glad you liked
the book!

Mark R Probst

Edited by The Threepenny Editor

ISBN: 978-0-9797773-0-1

LIBRARY OF CONGRESS CONTROL NUMBER: 2007904980

Published by Cheyenne Publishing
Camas, Washington
Mailing Address: P. O. Box 872412 Vancouver, WA 98687-2412
Website: www.cheyennepublishing.com

Acknowledgements

Special thanks to all those who encouraged me to keep trying:
Judy F., Lisa J., Ron M., Sharon S., and my biggest fan Jill P.
Also, I must express much gratitude to my editor, Sarah Cypher,
who taught me so much, whose insight was a godsend,
and whose numerous contributions
raised this story to a new level.
Thanks also to Judy Blackburn and Jeff Albaugh
for their generous contributions.
And finally a very special thanks to Tim,
who is my true inspiration.

Preface

I have always been a fan of the Hollywood western:
the films of John Ford, Anthony Mann, John Wayne,
and Jimmy Stewart, among many others. I had a
great desire to pay tribute to this genre of a more
glamorous and adventurous west. Later years would
bring about grittier and more realistic depictions, but I
still loved the romanticized films of the nineteen
forties and fifties. I have also had a great fascination
in how gay men and women were able to cope and
survive in different eras. E. M. Forster's *Maurice*
beautifully demonstrated how this was accomplished
in Edwardian England, and Gordon Merrick's *The
Lord Won't Mind* showed us what gay life was like in
1930s New York. I have chosen to write a story
intertwining these two concepts: thus a gay western.
History records very little about how homosexuals
existed in the old west, therefore much of what I write
is simple speculation. So in this work I hope to
achieve the *flavor* of the classic movie western
without the constraints of the old Hollywood taboos.

The First Part:
The Cowboy

Chapter One

The little bell hanging above the door gave a little jingle. Ethan looked up from the bins of oats he was restocking in back just as the stranger stepped in out of the bright sunlight. He stood for a few seconds, blinking into the gloom. Spotting Ethan, the man flashed him a toothy grin and said "Howdy." Ethan nodded. The stranger was in his early twenties, a somewhat tall cowboy with a lean build, a handsome face, square jaw, smooth skin tanned from the range, and a soft intelligence in his blue eyes as he continued to look at Ethan.

"Howdy, stranger! What can I get for you?" Mr. Simpson emerged from the back room, reading glasses on the end of his nose and a pencil tucked behind his ear. He was fifty-five, thin and sallow. He had probably been going over the day's receipts, accounting for every last nickel.

"Well, if it's not too much trouble I needed to get a few supplies." The cowboy seemed awfully polite and well mannered. He wasn't dirty, smelly, rough, rude or rowdy. His shirt wasn't wrinkled. His chaps and boots were clean. He was clean shaven. When he removed his hat, his hair was neatly cut, straight and blond, the kind of blond that had been bleached out by months in the sun.

"I need a quarter pound of coffee," he said, "a quarter pound of sugar, uh, five cans of beans. Do you have pickled eggs?"

"Yep." Mr. Simpson scribbled the order on a sheet of paper, "Anything else?"

"Some beef jerky, uh...canned peaches? Make that two cans, and a loaf of bread if you have it."

"Sorry, no bread," said Mr. Simpson. "We have flour and yeast and salt if you want to make your own."

"No thanks." He smiled again. "I also need some matches, and I'll take one of these newspapers here."

Ethan hefted up the sixty pound sack of oats and started for the storeroom. There were boys half his age who could haul as much or more, but he had been a bookworm for the better part of seventeen years and a general store clerk for the better part of nine months.

"Ethan, come gather up these items." Mr. Simpson held up the list. Ethan dropped the sack in the corner and timidly crossed to the front counter. The stranger was about his height and made direct eye contact, flashing another smile. Ethan faintly smiled back, took the list from Mr. Simpson and trudged to the back of the store to gather the goods.

"Are you new to town, stranger?" Mr. Simpson asked as he scooped the coffee into a small bag atop a scale.

"I'm just passing through," the cowboy replied. "I'm really hoping to find work as a ranch hand."

Ethan returned to the counter with an armload. He lined up the five cans of beans in front of Mr. Simpson. He glanced at the cowboy, who again made brief eye contact, this time with a slighter smile, before turning back to Mr. Simpson.

"You know," Mr. Simpson stroked his chin, "as it so happens, the Haywood Ranch is getting ready for the big cattle drive to Cheyenne in June."

"Really!" The cowboy grinned at Ethan as he deposited the canned peaches and pickled eggs on the countertop. "Could you give me directions on where to find this ranch?" The man looked so directly at Ethan that he wasn't sure if the question was meant for him or Mr. Simpson.

"Well, you go straight up the main street here, sir," Ethan answered, pointing at the north wall of the store. "And at the end of town you will see a road. Go east on that road and you will pass six homesteads. And you will come to a big spread called the Haywood Ranch. You can't miss it." He ducked away and retrieved the remaining supplies, and hovered nearby while the man neatly arranged and packed the merchandise into a burlap sack. Mr. Simpson tallied the sum on the same piece of paper upon which he had made the list, and quoted the total to the cowboy, who plopped down the appropriate coinage and picked up the sack.

The cowboy winked at Ethan and tipped his hat to Mr. Simpson. "I'm much obliged sir."

"Think nothing of it. What's your name stranger?"

"I'm Travis Cain. Glad to have met you." He extended his hand.

"I'm Mr. Simpson, the proprietor of this store. Good luck to you." They shook hands and Travis gave one last glance at Ethan before the door closed and the bell jingled. Ethan watched through the window as Travis took all the merchandise out of the burlap sack and packed it all carefully into his saddlebags. He mounted a beautiful sorrel mare, clicked his tongue and trotted off toward the Haywood Ranch.

*   *   *

Later that evening, Ethan hunched on a crate in the storeroom, engrossed in *Wuthering Heights*. He had been studious in school, so much so that he finished the twelfth grade at age fifteen. He had learned everything Miss Peet could teach him. Even now, two years later, he was quite close to her. The township didn't have anything so luxurious as a lending library – the nearest one was forty miles east, in San Antonio – so the only way he could get books was by borrowing them from Miss Peet. She had a modest collection and he had only a few more chapters to go in Brontë before he exhausted it. There were a few volumes that didn't interest him, but every so often she acquired new ones. If he could finish Brontë tonight, he could stop by Miss Peet's house on the way home from work tomorrow, return it, and see if she had anything new for him.

> *Mr. Heathcliff paused and wiped*
> *his forehead; his hair clung to it,*
> *wet with perspiration; his eyes*

*were fixed on the red embers of the
fire –*

"Ethan! Are you about done in there?"

Ethan slammed the book shut. "Just finishing up, Mr. Simpson!" He grabbed the broom and scurried up the stairs back into the store. It was six o'clock, closing time, and it would take him about twenty minutes or so to sweep up the spilled oats and red adobe dust from well-worn, creaky, hardwood floor. After he finished, he grabbed his book and a couple of mushy looking apples from the storeroom, and headed out the door. He had an understanding with Mr. Simpson about the apples. Customers preferred the prettiest, freshest apples, so the ugly ones often didn't sell. So Mr. Simpson agreed that he could take two of the bad ones everyday to feed the horses.

On the way home he passed by the town stables. There were two horses standing by the fence waiting for him. They whinnied as they saw him come around the bend. This was a daily routine that they looked forward to. He fed them each an apple, patted their noses, and stroked their manes. His father had taught him to ride when he was six – after he had been killed in a gunfight some nine years ago, his mother, Ophelia, had to sell the horses, and they hadn't owned any since. Occasionally some of the townsfolk let him ride theirs, and after ten years he had good horsemanship skills. If he could just save enough money, he might buy his own colt or filly. He wanted to get a young horse, form a special bond, and train it from the beginning. Not one that had been spoiled by a previous master.

The horses grunted their approval. The apples were gone, and when they saw he had no more, he headed for home.

He lived two miles from town. It was a small farm, just two cows, two dozen chickens and a small crop of potatoes, carrots and corn. William did all the farming and it was the only productive thing he did. William was bitter, and every so often repeated his oath over dinner to avenge his father's death by killing the man who murdered him. He had dropped out of school right after their father's death, around age twelve, to take over the farm. It was plenty of time to turn into a hard drinking, gambling ruffian. Lately he was getting locked up in the jail for stirring up trouble, but the sheriff had been close friends with Jack and Ophelia and always managed to get the injured parties to drop the charges.

Neither son made very much money, for different reasons, so Ophelia had turned the homestead into a boarding house. They were able to take as many as four boarders at a time. Meals and laundry service were included for twelve dollars a month. Currently they had three boarders – Mr. Pendegast, Mr. Baker, and Mr. Ponce. They were all cut from the same cloth. Like almost all of previous boarders, they were bachelors who had the misfortune of being short, pudgy, and balding men, and Mr. Pendegast and Mr. Ponce wore glasses. In Ethan's opinion, their problem was not that they couldn't find wives if they wanted to; they just aimed too high in the looks department. The kind of women who interested them would marry them only if they could offer ironclad wealth. Without it, they would have to accept somebody homelier, or do without. They chose the latter. And without wives, the motherly services of Ophelia Keller were an appealing alternative.

Mr. Pendegast worked in the town bank as a teller. Like Ethan, he walked to work. He left before Ethan in the mornings, but quite often Ethan would pass him on the way. Mr. Ponce and Mr. Baker were more of a mystery. They each did odd jobs way out of town. Since their work required a lot of traveling, they each had a horse and a rig. Care for their horses was their own responsibility.

Avoiding piles of mushy green horse manure, Ethan followed the deeply rutted road over the narrow bridge spanning the dry creek bed, passed the giant cottonwood tree, and rounded the bend to home. The Keller homestead was a long, spread out farmhouse with an upstairs loft over the kitchen that was used mainly for storage of Ophelia's sewing and quilting materials. When their father was alive, there were only four bedrooms, but sometime after Ophelia opened it to boarders, she had two more rooms built on. It had six bedrooms, a drawing room, a dining room, and a kitchen with a water pump that came up through the floor. Ophelia and Willie each had their own bedroom. The other four were for the boarders. In the event that all four rooms were rented out, Ethan was banished to the loft. But as one room was currently vacant, Ethan was using it. The bed was so much more comfortable than the little cot in the loft. There was also a nice sized barn with enough stalls for the cows and horses. Mr. Ponce and Mr. Baker also used the barn to park their rigs. There were also two outhouses. The second one was added at the same time the extra rooms were built.

As usual his mother had supper prepared and waiting. As he came in and kissed her on the cheek, she called for Willie, Mr. Pendegast, Mr. Ponce and Mr. Baker to come to supper. Everyone seated themselves around the dinner table. Tonight they were having jackrabbit stew and biscuits. As they often did, Mr. Ponce, Mr. Baker and Mr. Pendegast discussed politics. Tonight's subject was the effectiveness, or ineffectiveness based on your point of view, of President Rutherford B. Hayes. They were now debating whether or not Congress was right to override Hayes's veto of the Bland-Allison act. Ethan blocked them out, wondering if Heathcliff was actually going to force Cathy to marry his son. Later in the summer, when the sun didn't go down until eight o'clock he would sit on the porch and read, but now in early April, the sun had already gone down and so he would read by lamplight in his bedroom.

They had just finished the meal and Ophelia started gathering the plates. She had fair, smooth skin that hadn't aged since Ethan's earliest memory of her. She had Ethan's brown eyes, but her hair was jet black and curly. She kept it pulled back into a neatly arranged bun, and all around her hairline were rebellious wisps of curly hair. Even though they were untamable, they were attractive and she jokingly called them "poppies" because they just popped out on their own. In the years since she had reached middle age, she had put on a more robust look.

"Is everyone ready for dessert?" she asked. "There's apple pie." Ophelia's pies were the best in the region. She brought the pie out from the kitchen. It looked enticing – its lightly browned crust with crinkled edges and apple filling oozing out of the slits on top. All the men watched intently as she cut it into eight perfectly symmetrical slices. Ethan forgot about Heathcliff and Cathy. His slice was coming – but oh, who was knocking at the door so late? His mother looked worried, so he jumped up to answer it.

It was Willie's friend, Jim.

"Is Willie home?"

"Yeah. He's in the dining room."

Jim came in, brushed past Ethan and went to the kitchen. Of all Willie's friends, Jim, dark good looks, a lean build, short brown hair and a neat mustache, had the manners of a cowpoke, the meanest heart, and the most influence over Willie.

"Hey Willie," he said, ignoring everybody else, "you wanna go into town and start up a card game?"

"Sure, Jim. Just let me finish my pie –"

"Oh, Willie! No!" Ophelia cried. "Please don't go into town tonight. I'll worry myself sick. Please stay home."

"Ma! I'm going," he answered with a stern look. "Don't coddle me. Sit down and have a piece of pie, Jim. It's the best apple pie you'll ever taste."

Jim sat down and grabbed a slice of pie from Ophelia. He didn't bother to thank her before wolfing it down. Ethan quietly picked up his own slice of pie and was about to head for his bedroom to eat it while he read.

"Wait a minute, Ethan," Ophelia said, "I would feel so much better if you would go with your brother into town tonight."

"Ma," groaned Ethan, "I wanted to finish my book tonight."

"It would set my mind at ease." The look on her face turned the suggestion into an order.

"Sure, little brother" Willie said. "Come with us. We'll have a good time. Teach you how to play poker."

His mother was counting on him, and he was not one to disappoint his mother. There was no getting out of this one.

After dessert, Jim went outside to wait and Willie went into his bedroom to get his gun belt and coat. The three boarders, having paid no attention to the domestic banter of the Keller family, retired into the drawing room still engrossed in their political debate.

Ophelia turned to Ethan. "Sweetie, I'm counting on you. Please keep Willie out of trouble. I just couldn't take it if he ends up in jail again."

"I'll do my best, Mom."

"I won't worry near so much, knowing I can count on you."

The moon had just risen, so there was plenty of light to see their way, and it would still be up when they returned later. Had it been a moonless night or overcast, they would have needed a lantern. The glow of the moon turned the stones in the road to silver and the dust to blue. The only sounds were the light rustling of the brush in the breeze and the crickets.

A stranger would know right off the bat that Willie and Ethan were brothers. They were both the same height, about five-ten, and had the same smooth, fair skin. The only difference was that Willie had inherited his mother's curly black hair, which hung in ringlets all over his head, and hard work on the farm had made him brawny.

"Well, little brother, we're going to make a man out of you tonight. Get you drunk and get you a woman!" Jim joined Willie's laughter, hooted and playfully punched Ethan in the shoulder.

Ethan hoped he would be able to fulfill his promise to his mother, but if they had it in their mind to get drunk, he didn't know what he would be able to do to stop them.

"Bet you ain't never had you a woman, have you, little squirt?" sneered Jim.

Ethan didn't answer. They left the path and headed in a completely unfamiliar direction. They came upon a little shack. Lights shone out of the windows and the gaping holes in the roof, and Ethan heard the sound of children crying inside. Jim rattled the door. A young man opened the door and stepped outside: Willie's other friend, Horace.

A woman shrieked, "That's right get out! Get out and stay out! Don't come back 'til you have some money!" The children cried even louder. Horace stomped off to a little shed that was attached to the side of the shack and grabbed his gun belt from inside. Together the four of them made their way back to the path towards town.

Horace had long, unkempt, dirty hair, a pitiful ugly face with a mouth that always hung open, and a broken spirit. He was kind of like a dog that had been beaten as a puppy – he was subdued, and was mainly a follower. Jim was clearly the leader of the gang, and Willie fell somewhere in between.

"Hey, did you guys hear about that gunfighter in San Antonio?" Jim asked, "This guy killed four men in a gunfight! Can you imagine that? Four men! That is really fast shootin'."

"Damn fast!" said Willie. "I sure would like to meet a man like that. When I get me a Colt .45, I'll be able to shoot fast, too. This gun I have now can't shoot straight for shit. But when I get a Colt .45, you can bet, when someone tries to draw on me, BAM! I'll shoot him right between the eyes!"

"Yeah," Horace piped in, "then he'll be sorry."

"Damn right he will," said Willie. "You can bet he'll think twice before ever drawin' on me again!"

"I can't believe that gunfighter killed five men in one fight!" said Horace. "I sure would like to meet a man like that."

Idiots, thought Ethan. If anyone ever drew a gun on these three, they would piss their pants and go running for the hills.

They arrived in town and made their way to the saloon. On the main street was the general store where Ethan worked, the hotel and restaurant on one side of the street, and the saloon on the other side. Tonight, it was filled with cigar smoke. All the tables in the middle of the room were packed, and saloon girls bustled around serving drinks with coquettish hospitality. Along one wall was the bar, and the barkeep doling out shots of whiskey and mugs of beer for a line cowboys – it was a busy night. At the front of the saloon was the piano player, banging out music on an out-of-tune piano. In the back, tucked away in the corners to avoid the bustle, were three poker games going on. This saloon was not as nice as some of the ones in San Antonio, where there was a whole room in the back where gamblers could retreat for quiet games. Jim led them up to the bar.

"Four whiskies," Jim said to the barkeep.

"Um, make mine a sarsaparilla," said Ethan. Strong liquor burned his throat going down. Beer was more palatable to him, but he had a promise to keep to his mother.

"He'll be having a whiskey with the rest of us," said Willie. "It's time for you to start living a little."

He was not going to get anywhere bucking his brother, and

the barkeep knew it. He poured four shot glasses full of whiskey. "Leave the bottle," Jim said, and both he and Willie threw down at least two dollars in coins. The barkeep set the bottle down in front of them and turned away to help other patrons. They all knocked back their shots and Ethan choked on his as it went down. Willie filled the four glasses again. The three of them knocked back their second shots and watched Ethan, daring him not to follow suit. Reluctantly, he picked up the glass and poured the second dose down his throat. It went down easier. Willie filled Ethan's glass again, then he, Jim and Horace made their way to the back of the room to see if they could cut into one of the poker games.

Ethan stared at his glass. A tingly sort of euphoria crept into his head. He looked around. Nobody was paying him any attention. Without even thinking, he picked up the glass and downed his third shot of whiskey. That felt good. As drunkenness began to overtake him, he turned on the barstool to face the room. The men seated at the tables were truly having a good time. Some of them would get grabby with the saloon girls, who giggled and pulled away. They knew it was their job to keep the customers happy, so they were sure to giggle. Then Ethan observed the piano player, plinking away on the ivories. Gosh, that looked like fun. He wished he could play the piano. Well why not? He was feeling liberated, so he slid off his barstool, caught himself, and weaved his way over to the piano. He came up next to the piano player, and was transfixed on those fingers flying all over the keyboard. Wow. That looked like so much fun. He lunged forward with his hands and landed on the keyboard, but his fingers wouldn't go. His hands just flapped up and down making jarring piano sounds. The piano player was forced to stop and remove Ethan from his domain.

"Whoa there fella, just sit back and listen okay? I don't need any help here."

"But... I.... wanna.... play too!"

The piano player guided him to a nearby chair and then returned to his keyboard.

Saloon doors had those funny little spring hinges that caused them to bounce back every time somebody went through them.

Coming in or going out. What made them do that? He made it to the doors and put his head down to examine the hinges. CRACK! The door nearly knocked him senseless, but miraculously, his head didn't hurt.

"Whoa there little brother." Willie's voice was behind him. "You're feeling good now, aren't you?" Willie pulled him up by the armpits, put one of Ethan's arms around his neck, helped him walk to the back of the saloon, and sat him down in a chair. "Now you just sit here and watch me play poker. And be real quiet." Willie sat back down at his table. "Sorry guys, my brother needed a little help."

The three men with whom Willie was gambling frowned and glanced at one another in minor annoyance. For the next half hour, Ethan did as he was told and watched quietly. He didn't understand the rules of poker, but more often than not, Willie would reach out and scoop the chips from the middle of the table toward himself, and then carefully stack them with the ones he already had. His pile of chips was growing bigger and bigger. One of the gamblers grumbled; his big handlebar mustache looked like it was carved of wood. The cigar smoke seemed to dance its way around Willie's cards. Was is possible that the queen of hearts had just tilted her head and smiled? Ethan felt drowsy.

There was some sort of commotion. "I don't like the way you play cards mister!" Willie was shouting.

"Boy, that sounds an awful lot like an accusation. I don't think you want to be saying that."

"Nobody's that lucky!"

"I think maybe we should step outside," the gambler said in a calm voice. But Willie leaped up, overturned the table and took a big sloppy swing at the man, barely missing the man's jaw. Jim and Horace took this as their cue to jump in to the fray. Men brawled, throwing punches, shoving each other into walls, overturning more tables, and breaking liquor bottles. Ethan tried to stay out of the way and finally ducked down under a table to protect himself. The barkeep tried to break it up but only managed to get himself punched in the nose. Somebody must have gone for help, because suddenly there was gunfire.

21

Everybody stopped fighting and looked towards the door. There stood the source of the gunfire, the town deputy, a lanky man with about three days' growth of whiskers and scowl on his face. "What's this all about?" he said, "Who started this?" The barkeep came forward holding a bloody handkerchief to his nose. "It's them four, deputy. They got drunk and started beatin' on these men, with no cause." Ethan had crawled out from under the table and was surprised to find himself included in the accusation.

"Okay, you four," the deputy directed. "Hand over your guns. We're going to see the sheriff." The three of them handed over their guns in submission. Jim didn't look too pleased about it, and of course Ethan didn't have a gun. The deputy ushered them through the door and to the town jail, which was not on the main street in town. It was located one street over, straight across from the bank.

It was a simple little jailhouse with bars on the windows, a desk for the sheriff, a cot for whoever was on duty, a pot-bellied stove with a pot of coffee on top, a locked-up gun rack and three small cells in the back. The sheriff was a fat old man who looked very tired and weathered. He looked up from the papers that had been occupying his time and let out a groan as the four of them and the deputy came through the door.

"Oh Jesus, not again! Honestly, you boys are going to be the end of me yet. What did they do this time, Emmet?"

"Drunkenness, and bar fightin'."

"Any damages?"

"Minor. No one's pressin' charges anyhow."

"Okay, pour some coffee, Emmet. Let's get these boys sobered up."

Emmet poured black, thick-as-mud coffee into four tin cups. Ethan was glad for his. He wanted his head clear so he could understand what was going to happen to him.

"Jim, Horace, and William, I've tried to keep you guys from going down this path you're determined to take." The sheriff folded his arms, "I'm warning you, if you keep going the way you're headed, you're going to wind up on the end of a noose. Ethan, as for you, quite frankly, I'm shocked. I've never known you to be anything but a good kid. I was a good friend to your father, and always felt it my responsibility to look after you and William. I'm afraid he would be disappointed if he could see you now. And what's your mother going to say?"

"Well, do you have to tell her, sir?"

The sheriff just shook his head. "Jim and Horace, I don't have much hope for either of you. But William, please come to your senses and stop hanging around these two. Make your daddy proud, son." Willie jiggled his tin cup to make the coffee swirl around inside, and broke eye contact every time the sheriff's eyes met his. Jim glared at the sheriff. Horace hung his head and wouldn't make eye contact. After several cups of coffee and another forty-five minutes of the sheriff's sermonizing, their guns were returned to them and they were free to leave.

Ethan thought they ought to be deliriously thrilled at their luck and would go home at once. Outside the jailhouse, Willie and Jim's faces lightened up quickly and they holstered their guns, unfazed. Jim clapped Horace and Willie on the back. "Where to now, fellas?"

"We're not going home?"

"Not yet, little brother," Willie chided, "We've got someplace special to take you." Jim roared with laughter, and after a delay Horace joined in.

They walked the opposite direction to home, all the way to the other end of town, and then about a mile more to a remote two-story house. It was very nicely kept up – picket fence, flowers, neatly cut grass, fresh paint, and a small lamp shining out of one downstairs window. They went up to the door and quietly knocked. A portly, gray-haired woman opened the door.

"Come on in, boys," she said with a smile then called over her shoulder, "Girls! We got customers!" Ethan hung back by the door, but the other three leaned against the banister to patiently wait. A parade of six exquisitely groomed women of various shapes and sizes descended the stairs. They wore loose, flowing dresses made of colorful satins and silks, and their faces were painted like a doll's. The smell of perfume was overpowering. They immediately recognized three of their regular customers. "Who will it be, boys?" the gray-haired lady asked.

"I'll take Delilah," Willie responded, "and someone special for my little brother here. He needs a lot of tender lovin' care." Willie handed the gray-haired lady what looked like at least ten whole dollars. Surely he hadn't won that much gambling tonight. Jim and Horace each picked out their girl and raced upstairs to the bedrooms.

"I have just the girl for you, sweetie," she said to Ethan, "Dolores, come take care of this young man." A slender, ravishing, black-haired woman with long eyelashes and full red lips emerged from the remaining ladies and took Ethan by the hand. Her skin felt warm and smooth. Ethan wondered if she noticed that his palm was sweating. She daintily led him upstairs to a bedroom.

Ethan had often wondered about such things but this was not at all what he expected. Everything was so tidy. From the outside, it looked like a pretty country house. Who knew that inside it was full of fornication and adultery and who knows what other unspeakable things. It was actually kind of thrilling to witness.

Dolores took Ethan into the bedroom and closed the door. She gestured for Ethan to sit down on the bed, which he did, then she began to unbutton her dress, trailing her fingers against the lace at the neckline. She wore no undergarments, and the bare skin between her breasts was exposed and her wide nipples pushed at the satin. She bowed her head, and her raven hair fell across her slim cheeks and around her full burgundy lips.

"Please don't," he said.

"What's wrong, honey? Did you have something specific in mind?"

Ethan looked down at the floor.

"Oh, I understand," she said. Ethan blushed. "Don't worry honey, it's really easy. I'll show you what to do."

Ethan shook his head. "I'd rather not, if you don't mind."

"I'm already paid for, honey. You might as well get your money's worth. It'll only take a minute or two. Trust me. First-timers are always quick. Some of them finish their job before they even make it inside me."

Ethan felt his cheeks flush. His breath came fast and his stomach felt queasy. He looked away.

"If you don't mind I'd rather just wait here until my brother and his buddies are finished."

"Suit yourself. I don't mind. The money's the same if we do it or just talk." Efficiently, she buttoned her dress back up and sat on the bed. Ethan scanned the room. He wanted to say something but he couldn't think what. He focused his mind and finally said, "Do you live here? Or is this just where you work?"

"We all live here," she said. "It's part of the arrangement. We get free living quarters and food and we're paid well. It's really quite nice."

Ethan looked around the room. It was rather sparse, just a bed, a night table, a chair, a basin, and pitcher of water for washing up.

"This isn't your room is it?" he asked.

"Of course not," she laughed. "These rooms are just for doing business with the customers. We all have our own rooms with all our own things."

Ethan was impressed. It all seemed to be rather comfortable.

"How long are you going to stay here?" he asked, "I mean, do you ever plan to get married?"

"Married? Oh honey, men don't marry girls like me!"

"Why not? You're a very pretty lady."

"You're so innocent." She smoothed the wrinkles in her dress, her cheeks blushing ever so slightly. "That's just it. I'm not a lady, I'm a whore. And that's what I'll always be. But it's not that bad. I rather enjoy life here. When we're not working, there's plenty to keep us busy. Some of the girls knit and sew. We get to go on trips and shop, go horseback riding, go on picnics. We all have different hobbies. Pretty much anything we need or want is given to us." She waved her hand in the air as if her words could be dispelled like cigar smoke. "But let's not talk about me anymore. What's your story honey? What interests you?"

"Well," he said, "I like to read."

"Really? What do you read?"

"Oh, everything really. Dickens, Brontë, Austen, Verne."

"What are those?"

"They're authors. What do you read?"

"Dime novels mostly. I especially like *Belles and Beaux*. What else do you like?"

Ethan had so few interests. What could he bring up that would possibly be interesting to her? Well, there was the obvious. "I like horses."

"Really?" She shrieked. "I love horses! Stay right here. I want to show you something." She scurried out of the room.

While he waited, he looked around the room, this time noticing things he had missed. The sparse yellow wallpaper had some splotchy stains at the head of the bed. He could smell the lye in the cake of soap that sat by the water basin. Faint sounds of bumping and groaning escaped from a nearby room. He wondered if they might be Willie's groans. The image of Willie, naked on top of a pretty woman, was intriguing, but he couldn't quite grasp it.

Dolores returned with two large canvases attached to wooden frames. On them were oil paintings. One was of a beautiful dark brown Mustang mare with a white face and mane, and a lighter brown colt nursing at her side. She stood by a wooden fence in a grassy meadow and apple trees on a hill in the background. The other painting was of a white stallion on a hill, rearing up on his hind legs in front of an orange and purple sunrise and a herd of grazing mares in the meadow beyond.

"Golly, who painted these?" Ethan asked.

Dolores shrugged as if she didn't think they were very good. "I did."

"They're magnificent. You have a gift."

Dolores blushed. "Oh they're okay. Just something I do in my spare time." But she seemed to be captivated by the compliment, as women of her reputation rarely received them.

"What about you?" she probed. "You have eyes for some pretty girl in town?"

"Naw," he said, looking down at the floor. "There's no one."

"That's too bad. You're going to make some girl deliriously happy. And she'll be lucky to get you."

"Thanks," he said, "but after what happened to me and my brother tonight, I think a lot of girls would want to steer clear of me."

"Oh, you're just a darling!" She pinched his cheek. They could hear Willie's boots at the foot of the stairs. "Ethan! Aren't you done yet, little brother?"

"I'm coming! Just a minute!" he called back down. "Listen, can we just pretend we did it? My brother will never let me be if he knows I still haven't done it."

"As far as I'm concerned, you were a big ole stallion in bed!"

"Thanks," he grinned, "Goodbye." He bent over and gave her a sisterly peck on the cheek and went downstairs where his companions were waiting for him.

"Well how was she, little brother? Did she give you a good ride?"

"It was great."

Willie clapped him on the shoulder. "Now that we've made a man out of you, we can all go home."

Chapter Two

A week and a half after the notorious night out with Willie and his gang, Ethan still didn't know if the sheriff had told his mother. She had a way of pretending not to know about things she found upsetting.

One of the customers chuckled as he was about to leave. "Hey there, sonny, I heard about that ruckus you caused over at the saloon." His grown hayseed son said, "How many of them fellas you reckon you knocked out?" They both guffawed and went out the door.

Ethan had the thankless job of washing the store windows. It had been several months since their last cleaning and they were pretty dusty. The whole storefront was covered with windows, some of which were too high to reach without the aid of a ladder. That's where Ethan was now, lazily washing the inside high windows and eavesdropping while Mr. Simpson helped Miss Pinkerton and Miss Russell choose the right fabric to make a new spring dress. Miss Pinkerton and Miss Russell were two, stooped-over spinsters with angular bony features, wrinkles, and dewy eyes. Neither one had ever married and the two had lived together for as long as anyone could remember. When it came to dress material, they were fussy. They had unrolled and held up every single bolt of fabric, and they did not roll them back up, nor place them neatly back on the table. They just casually flung them aside into a messy pile, leaving Ethan his next job. After much fussing, and ignoring Mr. Simpson's opinion absolutely, they finally decided on a blue and white flowered print and asked for three yards. Mr. Simpson counted out three lengths of his outstretched arm from his fingertips to his nose. He then carefully cut it and wrapped it up for them.

While Mr. Simpson was finishing up the transaction, something outside caught Ethan's eye. It was that new cowboy riding up on his horse. He stopped in front of the store, hopped off his saddle, wrapped the reins around the hitching post and strode inside.

"Howdy, Ethan. How are you today?"

Ethan nearly fell off the ladder. He didn't even know that the cowboy knew his name.

"Hello. I'm doing fine." Ethan had to think hard. What was this cowboy's name? He should remember it. It wasn't that long ago.

"Hello Travis." Mr. Simpson called, "I'll be with you in a moment, just as soon as I'm finished helping these ladies."

Yes. That was it. Travis Cain.

Travis picked up one of the bolts of fabric and chuckled, tossing it aside. He put his hand on the side of that ladder as if to steady it.

"So I guess Mr. Simpson keeps you pretty busy here huh?"

"Yep." Good Lord, why couldn't he think of something to say?

"Do you live here in town?"

"My family has a farm and boarding house just a couple of miles out."

"Very nice," Travis said smiling, "It looks like I'm going to be sticking around here. I got hired on at the Haywood Ranch. I just came by to thank Mr. Simpson for sending me over there."

Ethan nodded. He still didn't know what to say. Miss Pinkerton and Miss Russell were now making their way out of the store, now fussing over whether or not they had made a hasty choice. Mr. Simpson shook Travis's hand.

"Good to see you again, Travis."

"Thank you sir. And once again I wanted to tell you that I'm obliged to you for sending me over to the Haywood Ranch. They hired me on."

Ethan went back to his window washing but tried to hear their conversation as they moved over to the front counter.

"Oh, good. Good. I'm happy to hear it."

"Yep," Travis continued, "this past week I've been mending fences, and rounding up some of the herd, and branding some of the calves, too. We'll be heading off on the cattle drive the first of June."

"That so," said Mr. Simpson. "How many head of cattle do they figure on driving up this year?"

Ethan mindlessly wiped back and forth, causing big, ugly streaks; he didn't notice because he was straining to hear what Travis was saying.

"The foreman, Mr. Bennet, reckons there will be between a thousand to twelve hundred. Right now there's only four of us signed on, but they're going to need at least fifteen vaqueros to drive the herd. They say as we get closer to June more cowboys will show up who were part of last year's drive."

"Good, good" Mr. Simpson nodded.

"I'm really looking forward to the drive," Travis said with a sigh. "I love traveling this country – seeing all the beautiful land and sleeping under the stars."

Ethan finally realized he was only making the windows worse, so he scurried down the ladder, dunked the rag in the water bucket, and scurried back up.

"Well, I hear drivin' cattle's pretty hard work," Mr. Simpson warned, "I don't think there's a whole lot of time for sightseein'."

"I've been on plenty of cattle drives. I've learned to admire the land while working."

"Well, good luck to you, lad. Is there anything I can get for you today?"

"Uh, sure. How about some of that licorice candy and a newspaper." He dug into his pocket, pulled out a couple nickels and paid for the candy.

"Have a good day now. I'll be seeing you around."

As he walked past the ladder he tipped his hat to Ethan. "I'll see you around too, Ethan." The bell above the door jingled, and

Travis mounted his horse and was gone.

*   *   *

On his way home, Ethan stopped to feed apples to the horses, then headed to the opposite end of town. He had just finished Dickens and could finally go see Miss Peet. She lived within sight of the schoolhouse in a cottage at the edge of town. She kept a tidy home – frilly, lace curtains; bright colored, fancy wallpaper; Oriental rugs; plush furniture; and all sorts of little trinkets like music boxes, crystal figurines and ceramic dolls. Everything smelled of lilacs. It was outrageously feminine, but Ethan loved its storybookish charm.

As always, she was thrilled at Ethan's unexpected visit. "Come in, dearie, and have some lemonade and cake." Miss Peet ushered Ethan into the house and went to go put on a kettle for their ritual discussion. Ethan was always glad for something sweet to eat, even though Miss Peet's cakes were nowhere near as good as his mother's. They tended to be leaden, but they were still sweet and Ethan wasn't picky when it came to dessert. He joined her into her kitchen and waited politely while she opened one of the doors of her exquisitely carved cupboards and pulled out two blue willow china plates and cups. She took a covered cake plate out of her pantry and a ceramic pitcher out of her icebox. The kitchen table was covered with a green and white plaid tablecloth, and she set their places with a mix of mindless routine and exquisite care.

"So how did you like this one?" she asked.

"Oh, it was just wonderful. The French Revolution and that evil Madame Defarge chopping off all those people's heads. I couldn't stop reading after Charles was sentenced to death."

"But tell me, Ethan, were you moved by the ending where just before Charles was to be executed, Sydney secretly switched places with him? He loved Lucie and her daughter so much that he made the supreme sacrifice for their happiness, by dying in place of her husband. I was moved to tears."

"Yes, I was moved." Ethan had wiped his eyes through the whole last chapter of the book, but he would never admit that to anybody, not even Miss Peet. "What I don't understand is, since these people were mistreated so horribly by the French

31

aristocracy and they were fighting for their freedom, why did they become so evil after they overthrew the government? I can sort of understand why they started beheading the aristocrats that had oppressed them, but why did they start killing innocent people like Charles? He had even renounced his family name and left the country, but because he was born into a family of tyrants, he was condemned."

"Well," explained Miss Peet, "throughout history the oppressed have often become the oppressors. Power definitely corrupts."

"I just can't imagine being condemned for nothing but the name you were born under. But I sure was glad when Madame Defarge got killed."

"Yes, it's always satisfying when the villain gets her due."

They finished their cake and Miss Peet took away the dishes. "Oh Ethan, I have something to show you. When I was in San Antonio last week, I bought something new. It was quite expensive and I feel so terribly guilty for having bought it, but I just couldn't resist. Just wait right here while I go and get it."

She departed into the bedroom and returned with a box between her hands. She sat down, opened the lid, parted the tissue paper, and carefully lifted out a music box shaped like a grand piano. It was made out of metal, decorated with gold and tiny little diamonds.

"It's beautiful." Ethan commended. She wound it up, opened the little piano lid and it began chiming a little tune. She handed it to Ethan and he studied it admiringly. They sat pensively listening to the music box. After a while Ethan spoke.

"There's a new cowboy in town."

"Really!" Miss Peet perked up. Even though she was in her thirties, she still hadn't given up on the prospect of marriage. She was attractive enough, with rosy cheeks, dishwater blonde hair, which she had arranged attractively in a cluster of curls on top of her head, and a shapely hourglass figure that was eminently noticeable through all her petticoats and girdles. Her problem was just that she was holding out hopes for a more refined and cultured man. Someone who shared her interests in literature, poetry, and art. And around these parts, such a man was nonexistent. But she was determined that somehow, some way, she would not become an old maid.

"He came into the store a couple of times. He's been hired on at the Haywood Ranch. He's a very nice man. Very friendly sort." Ethan reached over and picked up the music box.

"Well, do go on! Tell me everything about him."

"He's very polite and well mannered. He dresses neatly and he's very clean and well groomed, considering his job." He wound the key and the box started chiming again.

Miss Peet squealed with delight. "What's his name? How old is he?"

"His name is Travis Cain. I don't know how old he is. I would guess he's about twenty-four."

"And what does he look like?"

On this account Ethan was able to give her a vivid and complete description, from his hair and eye color, right down to his approximate shoe size. Had she been a sketch artist, she would have been able to create a wanted poster from it.

"Ethan, you must try and find out everything you can about this man. I must know if he's the one I've been waiting for all my life."

Ethan looked at her like she had just escaped from the loony bin.

"I don't know, Miss Peet. I'm kind of shy around strangers."

"Just find out what you can. Oh this is so exciting. I can't wait to meet him."

Ethan decided he had better be heading for home before his mother began wondering what had happened to him. "Thank you for the refreshments, Miss Peet. Do you have anything new for me to read?"

"Well I did pick up something new in San Antonio. I had you in mind when I bought it." She went over to the very large bookcase that nearly covered an entire wall of the parlor. It was filled with rows upon rows of leather-bound books. She pulled out a brand new volume and handed it to him. Jane Austen's "Pride and Prejudice."

Chapter Three

Occasionally, Mr. Simpson left Ethan in charge of the store. He would generally be gone for only an hour at a time, usually to make a deposit in the bank, make a delivery to a house-bound widow, or to send a telegraph. Ethan enjoyed these times because it made him feel important, and he took pride in the sales he made in Mr. Simpson's absence.

Mr. Simpson had only been gone about three minutes when Travis Cain walked through the door.

"Good morning, Ethan," he said in his cheerful, smiling way. "It's a beautiful day outside today."

"Good morning, sir." Feeling a jittery sensation in his stomach, Ethan moved to a position behind the counter.

"Oh please, call me Travis."

"Um, Mr. Simpson's not here right now but can I help you with anything... Travis?" He straightened the stack of receipts beside the register.

"Well, yes. Actually we guys over in the bunkhouse were looking for some sort of activity to pass the evening hours before going to bed. I was wondering if you had anything like that here in the store. Maybe a deck of cards?"

"No, I'm afraid we don't have any cards. But I'm sure you could get some from the saloon down the street."

"Well, what do you have?"

"We've got some books, if you like to read."

"No...I don't really go for much book reading. I prefer going out and experiencing life, rather than just reading about it." Ethan was perplexed. He looked around the store hoping to find the answer to Travis's dilemma.

"Oh, I know," he said, and took off for the back shelf. "How about a jigsaw puzzle?"

"Yeah," Travis agreed. "That's exactly the kind of thing I had in mind. Let's see what you've got."

Ethan led him over to where they kept the toys and showed him the puzzles. There were five different ones. Each was of a scenic picture and contained three hundred wooden pieces.

"Which one do you think is the prettiest?" Travis asked.

"I like the one with the horses," Ethan replied. "I'm crazy about horses."

"Really? Do you have a horse?"

"Not yet. I'm saving my money to buy my own colt or filly." He lowered his eyes and stared for a second at Travis's belt buckle. "I think your mare is beautiful."

"Thank you." Travis smiled and looked toward the window. "I've had her since she was a filly, four years ago. She was my very first horse." He picked up the puzzle box, fumbled with it, then placed it back on the shelf. "Would you like to ride her? Let's go out and take a look."

They went outside and Ethan patted her nose and stroked her mane. The jittery feeling drained away as contact with the mare gave him confidence. She whinnied in approval. Travis pulled some sugar lumps out of his pocket and fed them to her. She nuzzled his hand and moved closer to him. "Well, do you want to ride her?"

"I wish I could," Ethan said, "but I have to watch the store. Mr. Simpson would never forgive me if I left the store unattended."

"Oh. What time do you close up shop?"

"Six o'clock."

His face lit up with a grin. "Good. I'll come back again then and you can ride her. Now I'll just go ahead and buy the puzzle with the horses and be on my way."

*   *   *

All through the day he could think of nothing but the meeting he had arranged with Travis. He was even too excited to read. Finally six o'clock came. He had finished sweeping up and stood looking out the windows, waiting. Mr. Simpson stuck his head out of his office.

"Aren't you going home, Ethan?"

"Yep. I'm just waiting for someone. He's going to let me ride his horse."

Mr. Simpson grumbled something and returned to his accounting. Finally at ten minutes past six Travis rode up. Ethan bolted out the door.

"Hop on up," Travis said. "I'll take you somewhere where you can really ride." He took his foot out of one of the stirrups so Ethan could use it to hoist himself up. "You might want to hold on to my belt. I wouldn't want you to fall off before we get there." Ethan put his hands on Travis's hips and gripped his belt. Travis made a clicking noise with his mouth and the horse trotted off. Once out of town they sped up to a full gallop and went on for at least five miles. They arrived at a spot that Travis must have already had in mind – it was a nice grassy field nestled in some small hills. Ethan recognized this spot. The year before a small grove of trees had been felled to build an extension onto the schoolhouse. All that remained were a few scattered logs. Travis stopped beneath a big sprawling oak that sheltered them from the evening sun, and they both hopped down.

"Are you ready to ride her?"

"You bet," Ethan said. "What's her name?"

"Cleo. Short for Cleopatra."

Ethan climbed up into the saddle. He had expected the horse to be jittery, as they usually were with unfamiliar riders, but not Cleo. She might have been carrying Ethan all her life. He gently squeezed her sides with his heels and she smoothly trotted off. He leaned forward and she instinctively knew he wanted more speed, so off she went, like the wind. He lightly touched the right rein to her neck and she turned left with ease. She easily changed direction with the slightest pressure from his knees. She was like an extension of his own body. The slightest tension on the reins

36

and she would slow. Cleopatra was definitely the finest steed
Ethan had ever ridden in his life. He took several jumps over
logs and she sailed over them with complete confidence. He felt
like he was flying. After several laps around the field, he
returned to the oak tree, brimming over with enthusiasm.

"She is absolutely magnificent! I've never ridden a horse like
this before. I can't believe how well trained she is."

Travis grinned with pride. "Thanks. She does have a light
mouth."

"I'll say! And the smoothest gait of any horse I've ever
ridden. I barely even needed to use the reins." Ethan smoothed
her mane. "How do you get her mane to hang all on one side like
that?"

"I keep it cut short, and brush it everyday to train it to fall one
way. You've got the right idea about getting a colt," Travis said.
"That way, it won't be spoiled by any other owners. If you bond
to them when they are young, they will be completely devoted to
you."

"I'd be very lucky to have a horse this good. And she has
such a strong build. She must come from very good breeding."

"She does. I picked her out very carefully."

The sun was just starting to set and the shadows were
growing long.

"I had better be heading home for supper." Ethan said.

"I'll take you home," Travis offered. "Just show me where
you live."

They both mounted the horse the same way they had come,
with Ethan sitting behind and headed back to town.

"So, where are you from Travis?" he asked.

"Well my family lives in San Antone, though I don't stay
there much anymore. I've been traveling the country for the past
three years, working as a cowhand at different ranches and going
on cattle drives. I have three younger sisters. I adore them. They
all live on a farm with my parents. I try to get back to see them
every now and then." He momentarily switched the reins to one
hand so he could adjust his hat. "What about you? You said
your family runs a boarding house. Your father and mother..."

"My father is dead," Ethan interrupted. "It's just my mother that runs the boarding house."

"Oh, I'm so sorry."

Ethan could hear the pain in his voice. "Don't be. It was nine years ago. I was only eight at the time"

"Do you have any brothers or sisters?"

"One brother, Willie. He does all the farm work."

"Do you two get along well?"

"All right I guess. He kind of drives me crazy sometimes."

They were back in town now and Ethan pointed the way to his house. It was just getting dark as they rode up. Ethan hopped down.

"Thanks for letting me ride Cleo. I appreciate it."

"Think nothing of it, Ethan." Travis hunched over in the saddle. "Anytime you feel like riding come on out to the ranch. I'll be there 'til June and you can ride Cleo as much as you like."

"Gee thanks, Travis." He kept his hand on Cleo's flank.

"Sure, anytime. Be seeing you around!" It was getting dark, and he rode off at full speed.

Inside Ophelia was just putting supper on the table and Willie was sitting waiting to eat. "Who was that cowboy you rode up with Ethan?" she asked. She had been spying out the window.

"Just a friend from in town."

"What's this?" Willie piped up. "You got you a friend now, little brother? I'll be dog-gone! A real live friend? Not one of them make-believe friends from your storybooks?"

Ethan rolled his eyes. Willie's chiding was annoying but it didn't bother him anymore.

"He looked like a very nice boy," Ophelia said, throwing a reproving look at Willie. She didn't feel the same way about *his* friends.

Chapter Four

Ethan awoke on a Sunday morning in early May to the smell of coffee and frying bacon. He lay there for a while just taking in the aroma while the last of his sleep drained away. He got up and went to look out the window. The rain that had been pouring down the past two days was finally gone. And not a moment too soon – Sunday was the only day of the week he was guaranteed to have to himself. Mr. Simpson always closed the store on Sunday, it being the Lord's day and all. Also, he had big plans for today. He pulled on his clothes, made a quick trip to the outhouse and then came into the kitchen to see about getting some of that breakfast. His mother was in her apron mixing up batter for flapjacks.

"Good morning, sweetheart," she said. "Your brother never did come home last night. I'm starting to get worried. Do you know anything about where he might be?"

"No. But I'm sure he's just fine." Ethan poured himself a cup of coffee. "He's probably just passed out drunk somewhere, and now he's probably trying to sleep off a hangover."

"ETHAN!" Ophelia shrieked, setting down the bowl of batter and putting her hands on her hips. "How can you say such a thing?"

"Just being truthful, Mother."

"Can you do me a favor and go milk the cows, then put them

out to pasture?"

He was about to protest, then thought better of it. "Yes, ma'am."

"And gather up the eggs too?"

"Yes, ma'am." He picked up the milk pail and basket and trudged out to the barn. There were still a few clouds hanging around, but the sun pierced through. The whole outdoors smelled fresh and earthy. A light breeze caused the surrounding trees to shudder and release their raindrops. The mud enveloped the heels of Ethan's boots, making a plopping noise as he walked. He completed his tasks, then came back in for a hearty breakfast. It was just he and his mother, since the boarders usually got up very late on Sundays.

"What are your plans today, Ethan?"

"I was going to go over to the ranch and see if I could ride Cleo. Travis said I could come and ride her anytime I like." He hoped she wouldn't forbid it because of his careless remark about Willie.

"Good." Ophelia said, "Since you'll be going by the town anyway, could you please stop by the sheriff's office and see if he knows anything about Willie?"

"Sure, Ma. But I'm telling you he's just fine. I'm sure he'll be home before supper."

"I hope so. That boy's going to send me to an early grave."

After breakfast Ethan walked into town. He ambled along and enjoyed his day outside. He stopped by the livery stable to see the horses, then went to the sheriff's office. The freshly shaven deputy was sitting at the desk drinking coffee and reading the newspaper.

"Deputy Sloane?"

"Why, good morning, Ethan. What are you doing in town on a Sunday?"

"Good morning, sir. I'm looking for the sheriff."

"He's at home restin'. Did you need him for something?"

"Well, I was just wondering... have you seen Willie anywhere? He didn't come home last night and my mother's worried."

"Lost your brother, have you?" Emmett chuckled. "No I ain't

seen him. But I figure he's just passed out drunk somewhere."

"That's what I said."

"Tell your ma not to worry, he'll turn up soon. If I come across him, I'll dust him off and send him straight home."

"Thanks, deputy."

Ethan next went by the saloon to see if Willie was there, but the big doors behind the swinging saloon doors were closed and locked tight. Ethan looked in the window but only saw chairs stacked upside down on the tables, and the bar clean and polished. He couldn't think of any other place where Willie might be, so he let himself off the hook and headed over to the ranch.

Haywood Ranch was a three-mile walk from town, so with Ethan taking his time meandering through the mud, he didn't arrive until the sun was almost directly overhead. He knocked on the door to the bunkhouse but nobody answered. After several more attempts he decided to look around and see if he might find someone. The enormous barn still smelled of a fresh coat of white paint. There were more horse stalls lined up than he had ever seen in one place. Several horses snorted and stamped, but no other humans were present. He ambled over to the small building on the other side of the corrals. The top half of the door was open, so he peeked inside. It was the smithing shop. Horseshoes and irons were lined up on a table beside the bellows and anvil. The furnace was hot, but no one was tending it. As Ethan walked back to the bunkhouse, he saw Mr. Bennet, the foreman, coming down from the ranch house up on the hill. He was a large fellow, well over six feet tall and had a prizefighter's build. He wore a large silver belt buckle, scuffed suede boots with a broad cowboy hat shading his pudgy round face.

"Hello there. Is that...why yes...if it isn't Ethan Keller. Why I haven't seen you for years. You've done some growin', boy. Did you come to see the horses?"

"Well actually, Mr. Bennet, I was looking for Travis Cain. He said I could ride his horse."

"Oh yes, Travis. One of the new hands. He's out working on the north side – they're out building fences this morning. If you want to wait around, I'm sure they will be back for dinner."

"Thank you sir, I'll wait."

"Okay. Good to see you again." Mr. Bennet went about his business and Ethan sat down on the bench in front of the bunkhouse and waited, chewing on a length of straw and thinking about different horse names, just in case he ever got one.

Shortly after noon Travis and another man rode up to the bunkhouse on their horses. Both men had been working hard; they were drenched in sweat and there was mud all over their chaps and arms. Ethan had never expected he would see the cleanest cowboy in Texas looking like this. Travis removed his chaps and both men began washing their faces and arms in the water trough.

Travis made introductions while up to his elbows in the trough, water dripping off his face. "Don is one of the other ranch hands," he said. Ethan and Don nodded at one another. Don was rough, dirty, and unshaven – exactly the kind of cowboy Ethan was so used to seeing.

"I wondered if it would be okay if I rode Cleo today," Ethan said.

"Well of course you may," Travis replied. "But first come join us for some grub. There's plenty, and Don and the other guys won't mind." Don walked off. Ethan wondered whether he minded or not.

The bunk house was a large, single room building that housed about fifteen beds, all laid out around the walls. In one corner was a stack of cots for when they ran out of beds. A big long table crowded the middle of the room with eight chairs to a side and one on each end. Whoever was responsible for the big pot of simmering beef stew on the stove had set a basket of fresh bread on the table. Travis hung his hat on a coat hook, closest to a big cupboard that contained the plates, drinking glasses, silverware and red-checkered napkins. Two more dusty, rough-looking cowboys entered the bunkhouse, and hung their hats next to his. They were practically indistinguishable from Don, except that one of them had a nasty scar under his left eye and a fiercely mean turn to his lip. Ethan instantly disliked him. Travis introduced them as Joe and Fred. Fred was the one with the scar. Carrying two bowls, Travis sat down next to Ethan and placed the second in front of him. The sharp aroma of the stew's spices was enticing.

"Eat up. It's quite good. Bessie is the ranch cook. She makes wonderful beef stew," Travis explained. "Unfortunately she won't be going on the cattle drive with us, so we'll have to make do with whatever cook gets hired on to go with us."

"Yeah, cattle drive grub's fillin' but not very tasty," Don said.

"We could kidnap Bessie," Joe added. "Just tie her up and drag her along." They all laughed at the joke. Fred's raunchy laugh made Ethan shiver a bit.

"Once we leave the ranch, the first town we'll hit where you can get a decent meal is Pueblo," Fred said. "That's a good eight hundred miles. I've been on this trail before, and I can tell you it's mighty lonesome before Pueblo."

"I was on a drive once before on the Goodnight-Loving Trail," Travis said. "And I can tell you there are some long, uncivilized stretches."

"That'd be about right," Don said. "But the worst part is the beginning. The desert between the Concho River and the Pecos is just murder. But once you hit the Pecos, the trail follows the river north into New Mexico all the way to Fort Sumner."

Ethan and the four cowboys ate a big second helping, and after the meal, Travis cleared away the table and Ethan got up and looked around. On Travis's bed was a big flat square board, holding together the partially put-together puzzle.

"Bring it over here to the table," Travis said, "and you can help me work on it." Ethan moved it carefully and Travis sat down across from him. The entire border was finished, but only one horse's head on the side was put together. They worked on the puzzle while the other cowboys lounged around the bunkhouse.

"How are things going at the store?" Travis asked.

"The past few days, business has been really slow due to the rain. People just don't want to go out in bad weather. But it does give me time to catch up on my reading."

"Reading?" Travis raised his eyebrows. No doubt he was remembering his negative comments. "You like to read?"

"It's my favorite thing."

Travis glanced over at the other men, then dropped his gaze to the floor. "So what book are you reading now?"

"I just finished *Pride and Prejudice.*"

"Oh? And what was that about?"

"Well... It's about a sort of middle-class British family. There are four daughters and the mother is very determined to get them married off to successful gentlemen. The mother is very fussy and the father kind of calmly puts up with her. And the whole thing is just about the ordeal of finding husbands for these four girls."

"Hmm." Travis looked pensive. "And did these girls end up marrying who they were expected to marry, or did they marry for love?"

"Oh they definitely ended up marrying for love. Elizabeth, she was the main character, was proposed to by a man she didn't love and her mother went to pieces when she turned him down. But her father supported her choice and she ended up marrying the man she really did love."

"Good," Travis said. "Because I always think it's important that people marry for love."

The other three cowboys overheard this.

"So is that what you're doing Travis? Waiting for love?" Don teased. "And where do you expect to find her Travis? Out on the range?" All three cowboys burst out laughing.

"Yeah," Joe chimed in, "Travis thinks he's going to find his true love out on the cattle trail!"

"No wonder he keeps his clothes so neat and clean!" Fred added with just a touch of scorn in his voice. "He's waiting for his true-love fairy princess out on the dusty trail!"

Travis scoffed. "You three dung-beetles wouldn't know anything about love." He turned to Ethan. "So, do you want to go out and ride Cleo now?" Ethan nodded vigorously that he did.

"Go ahead and take her out. Don't ride her too hard. Take as long as you want and just sponge her down and brush her when you're through and leave her in the stable. We've got to get back to work now, but I'll see you again later."

Ethan rode Cleo most of the afternoon, exploring the ranch and feeling much like a king on the world's finest steed, when he happened across Willie making his way home on the road. He reined Cleo in and guided her to trot alongside his brother.

"Where've you been?"

Willie kept walking and didn't even take notice of the horse. "Mind your own business, little brother."

"You know Ma's been fretting."

Willie shrugged and kept walking. He was surely up to something, but Ethan knew he wouldn't get anywhere with direct questions, so he turned Cleo aside, squeezed her flanks and bounded away.

Chapter Five

The next day, Ethan decided to stop by Miss Peet's house after work to return *Pride and Prejudice*. Miss Peet greeted Ethan even more enthusiastically than usual, taking his arm and ushering him into the house for a sarsaparilla and little crackers with liverwurst. He handed her the book, but she tossed it aside and turned to face him directly.

"So tell me Ethan, what did you find out?"

"About what?"

"About Travis, of course, you silly boy."

"Oh." He was reluctant to tell her anything. He didn't understand why, but her intense interest in Travis bothered him. It was like she was trying to horn in on their friendship and he didn't like it at all. On the other hand he had agreed to find out what he could for her, so he recounted what new information he had and she memorized every word.

"Ethan, you must find a way to introduce me to Travis!" She lurched forward, her eyes protruding a little. "There must be some way we can meet. Let me think." She pressed her hand to her brow. "I know! You could invite Travis to your house for one of your mother's famous home-cooked meals, and I shall be one of the guests too! No, wait a minute, that wouldn't work. With he and I being the only invited guests, he would know right away that it's by design. It must seem like a purely coincidental meeting." She paced back and forth in front of her bookcase, absentmindedly fingering the volumes, then spun around on her heel with her finger in the air. "I've got it! You invite Travis home to supper, and then I will find some excuse to drop by your house, totally unaware that you have a guest. That seems perfectly innocent. He will be none the wiser."

In the midst of such underhanded and deceitful manipulations, Ethan felt like *he* was in a Jane Austen novel. If Travis were to find out he were a part of this set up, he would die of embarrassment.

"Miss Peet, I'd really rather not..."

"Oh Ethan, you must help me do this. It's really not that big a deal. If women didn't use their little tricks, men would stay single forever."

"Well... I don't know..."

"Listen, Ethan. It's quite simple actually, all you have to do is invite him over to supper on, let's say Friday evening. I'll arrange everything with your mother. See? Your part in the whole thing is very minimal."

"Okay," he agreed. "I guess I can do that. After all it would only be polite, considering all he's done for me, letting me ride his horse and all."

Miss Peet smiled victoriously. "Go over to the ranch tomorrow and give him the invitation and let me know if he's not able to make it, and I'll stop by and set things up with your mother." With that, Miss Peet hurried him out the door and on his way. She hadn't even given him a chance to discuss the book. He had, however, left out one crucial piece of information: that was Travis's belief that people should marry for love.

*   *   *

The plan went off without a hitch. The next day Ethan stopped by the ranch and invited Travis to supper. Travis was extremely pleased and gratefully accepted, suspecting nothing out of the ordinary, but by Friday evening Ethan was even more nervous about the whole affair. He imagined Miss Peet bursting in the door, lurching into Travis's lap and dropping broad hints about love and babies. At 6:05 there was a knock on the door. Ethan, dressed in his best Sunday suit and bowtie, answered the door. Travis looked fine as ever, his brown trousers and yellow cotton shirt neatly pressed. Ophelia was in the kitchen putting the final touches on the roast mutton. Mr. Pendegast and Mr. Ponce were playing a game of chess in the drawing room and Mr. Baker and Willie hadn't come out for supper yet. Ethan made the formal introductions and led Travis into the kitchen to meet his mother.

"It's a pleasure to meet you, Mrs. Keller," Travis said with a little bow. "The supper smells absolutely heavenly."

"Why thank you, Travis," she said, with an approving smile. "Just make yourself at home. Supper will be ready shortly."

They went back into the drawing room and sat down to wait for supper.

"This is a very nice boarding house," Travis said. "Are all the rooms occupied?"

"All except one. Mine."

"Yours?"

"Whenever there's a vacant room, I get it. Otherwise I get kicked up to the loft."

Travis gave a little chuckle. Willie came out of his bedroom to see if supper was ready.

"Travis, this is my brother, Willie. Willie, this is Travis Cain."

"A pleasure to meet you Willie." Travis extended his hand. Willie shook it and mumbled, "Much obliged." Willie had washed up for supper but was still wearing his work clothes. Obviously it didn't occur to him that it was customary to dress for supper when you had a guest.

They had just begun the meal when a knock interrupted them. Ophelia feigned curiosity. "I wonder who that could be?" Willie went to answer the door and retuned being followed by none other that Miss Peet herself. She entered the room lugging a big mantel clock.

"Why hello, Clara! Come right in." Ophelia stood up and approached her.

"Hello, Ophelia, Mr. Pendegast, Mr. Ponce, Willie, Mr. Baker, Ethan." There was a clatter of discarded forks and scraping of chairs as the men all stood and returned the greeting.

"And I don't believe I've had the pleasure of being introduced to this handsome stranger," she continued.

"Oh dear me, I'm so sorry!" Ophelia said. "Clara, this is Travis Cain, and Travis let me introduce you to Miss Clara Peet, our schoolmarm."

"Pleasure to meet you, ma'am."

"Why the pleasure's all mine, Mr. Cain."

"Please call me Travis, ma'am. Nobody calls me *Mr. Cain*."

"I will, Travis, and you may call me Clara. Oh dear, I've come at the most inopportune time. You're all just sitting down to supper. I had brought this mantel clock for Mr. Pendegast to fix. It seems to have quit working and he is so handy with mechanical things." Ethan knew for a fact that clock had not been working for at least a year.

"I'll take a look at it right after supper, Miss Peet." Mr. Pendegast's face glowed a healthy, damp shade of red from the compliment.

"Please, Clara, join us for supper," Ophelia said. "There's plenty to go around."

"Oh, no. I couldn't impose! I'll just be on my way."

"Clara I insist, you must join us."

"Well, if you *insist.*"

Ophelia got her a plate out of the cupboard and Ethan took her coat and pulled up a chair for her.

"Oh, Ophelia, this supper looks simply scrumptious! You are such a fine cook! My, oh my, what a layout this is. Are you enjoying your supper Travis?"

"Yes ma'am. It's quite delicious."

"So I take it you are a new boarder here?"

"Oh no. I'm just a guest."

"Of whom are you a guest?" she asked coyly.

"I'm a friend of Ethan's."

"Really!" she said. "Ethan was one of my finest pupils. As you know I'm the schoolteacher here in town, and Ethan and I have remained close even though he's completed school. I'm surprised he never mentioned you."

Ethan barely kept his jaw from dropping. After the initial shock, he thought better of her. At least the deception protected him.

"And what is it you do for a living, Travis?"

Ethan reddened. Was she ever going to let him have a bite? The poor guy's fork had been hovering for the last three questions.

"I'm a cowhand," he answered. "Or as we are commonly called around here, a vaquero. I generally go from ranch to ranch wherever help is needed. I've been on quite a few cattle drives in my life. Currently I'm working as a ranch hand at the Haywood Ranch. We are leaving in about three weeks to move the Haywood herd north to Cheyenne in the Wyoming territory." Seizing the opportunity, Travis took a big bite of food.

"Fascinating!" Miss Peet said, "but isn't it dangerous out there in the unsettled territories? I mean with all the savage Indians and all?"

Travis tried to chew his food quickly. Ophelia shifted in her chair a bit. Once he finally managed to swallow, he answered. "Well actually the trail is pretty well established now. There's very little Indian resistance. This particular route we are using is the Goodnight-Loving trail. They call it that because that was the names of the fellas who started it. Back then, maybe ten or eleven years ago, it was very dangerous. It was nine hundred miles of wild country. The Comanches lived there and they attacked the cowboys for invading their territory. In fact Mr. Loving was killed by Indians on their second cattle drive."

"Oh, my," Miss Peet said with great concern. "That's just terrible. You are so very brave to make that trip."

"Well, as I said it's much safer now. I very much enjoy traveling the country. I love the outdoors and nature."

"As do I!" Miss Peet said enthusiastically. "I'm a great lover of the outdoors."

That was certainly stretching the truth to the breaking point. Miss Peet hated the trips even to San Antonio.

Travis brightened. "There's nothing more peaceful than roaming this beautiful country and sleeping underneath the stars."

"But certainly, you intend to settle down somewhere, eventually? Perhaps get married and raise a family?"

"Someday I'd like to build a ranch, and raise horses."

Ophelia spoke up. "Clara, why don't you let Travis finish his supper? It's going to get cold."

Willie jumped up and brushed the crumbs off his lap.

"I'm heading out," he said to Ophelia. "I got stuff to do. I probably won't be back tonight, so don't wait up for me. And don't worry."

Ophelia looked like she was about to protest, but held herself back in front of the guests. "Don't you at least want your dessert?"

"I'm in a hurry. I'll just take it with me."

She went to the kitchen and brought him back a piece of pie wrapped in a napkin.

"I'll just take a look at that clock now," Mr. Pendegast said as he got up from the table.

"Oh yes, I would so appreciate it if you could fix it. I don't know what could have happened to it." Miss Peet turned her attention back to Travis. "A horse ranch. That does sound quite charming. Where might you decide to build this ranch?"

"Oh, I don't know really. I've always thought Colorado was a beautiful place, or maybe New Mexico. I've been all over this country, and it's really hard to decide where I'd like to end up."

"Well wherever it is, I'm sure the lucky lady you choose will be so happy to cook and clean for you."

Ethan had just about all he could take. "Ma, if I could be excused, I'd like to go out and see Cleo."

"Sure, honey. Go right ahead."

"I'll go with you," Travis said, jumping up. Miss Peet looked a little bit startled, like she had just been slapped in the face. But Travis took no notice of her and he and Ethan escaped outside.

The cool night air smelled fresh. The quietness was serene. Cleo was tied to the hitching post in front of the porch. Ethan fed her a few sugar lumps and stroked her mane, and was rewarded with a nuzzle. Travis sat down in the rocking chair on the porch. The sun had just gone down and the first stars were beginning to twinkle in the dusk.

"It's a beautiful night." Travis clasped his hands behind his head and propped his legs up on the banister.

"Yep." Ethan climbed up on Cleo and patted her neck. He

just wanted to sit on her for a while. "Willie's up to something. I just know he's getting involved in something bad. Did you notice the way he was acting tonight?"

"Sort of." Travis shrugged. "He did look like a man with a guilty conscience. You don't have any idea what it could be?"

"No."

"Can't you find out? Maybe ask him?"

"He wouldn't tell me anything. I don't think he would trust me."

"Oh well. I suppose time will tell." He took in a deep breath and exhaled slowly. "It's getting pretty dark. I should probably offer to escort the schoolteacher home."

"Don't bother doing that. She's perfectly capable of looking after herself. She travels alone at night all the time."

"Still, it would only be polite."

Ethan didn't want Travis to be alone with Miss Peet. It was just a feeling he had. Maybe jealously? "You know, I think she has eyes for you."

Travis chuckled. "Well, yeah. Even a blind man could see that."

"So do you want to court her?"

"Nah. I have some other plans in mind. Rest assured, I will not be courting the schoolmarm."

Ethan felt great relief. Miss Peet had no hold on Travis. Their friendship was safe.

"Well, go ahead and escort her home. Like you said, it would only be polite."

They sat out in the dark, Ethan on the horse and Travis in the rocking chair. Travis whistled a merry little tune and Ethan looked up at the night sky, studying the stars. After a while they went back inside. Mr. Pendegast had the mantel clock all taken apart and was looking perplexed about the whole thing. Ophelia and Clara had cleared the table and were hashing through the latest town gossip. Mr. Ponce was reading a newspaper and Mr. Baker had evidently retired for the evening.

"Are you boys ready for your dessert now?" Ophelia asked.

"Yes ma'am," Travis answered, "and Miss Clara, I would be honored to escort you home tonight, if you wish."

Miss Peet blushed to the roots of her hair. She obviously thought she had made a conquest. Ophelia smiled her approval as well. Only Ethan knew that Miss Peet was going to be very disappointed.

Chapter Six

About a week later, Ethan and Mr. Simpson had one of those days where it seemed just about everybody in town needed something from the general store. While Mr. Simpson added up the bills, wrote the receipts, and collected the money; Ethan ran around the store gathering up pickles, jerky, lamp oil, and wheat germ. He was hoping that business would slow down so he could take a break. Instead, Miss Peet showed up.

"Ethan! How are you doing today?"

"On my toes, Miss Peet."

"That just means lots of money for Mr. Simpson," she joked. "I've come to look in the catalogues and see if I can find a tea set to my liking."

Ethan waited for the nearest customers to drift away and when he saw that Mr. Simpson wasn't looking, he sidled up close to Miss Peet. "So how did it go with Travis, the other night?"

"Well," she said with a hint of reservation. "He seems a little on the shy side. It's going to take some time to warm him up to the idea of courtship. But as God is my witness, I'll get through to him. And before you know it we'll be courting, and then it won't be long until you hear wedding bells."

She certainly was optimistic. Far be it from him to end this little fantasy. "Well I hope so, Miss Peet, and I hope you find a tea set you like. Maybe you'll be coming back soon to pick out curtains and china patterns!"

"You never know!" she said. "I'll just go see what I can find and you keep up the good work." She made her way through the small crowd of people up to the counter to look through the catalogues.

About ten minutes later Travis came through the shop door. The crowd had thinned down to a half a dozen people, including Miss Peet. She was still looking at pictures of tea sets with Mr. Simpson. Travis must have seen her, but he made his way directly to Ethan. There was no doubt whom he had come to see, but when Miss Peet looked up and saw his broad shoulders and clean shirt, she called out immediately.

"Oh, yoo-hoo, Travis! What a pleasure it is to see you again so soon!"

"Miss Clara." He removed his hat and nodded at her. "How are you today?"

"I'm doing just fine. And you?"

"I'm doing well. Good day to you ma'am." And with that he turned away and proceeded to talk with Ethan. Miss Peet looked miffed, but then decided it just must be due to his shyness around women and went back to her catalogues.

"Ethan I've come here to ask you an important question."

"I needed to talk to you about something too."

"Really? What?"

Ethan lowered his voice. "Well, I found out what Willie's been up to. The morning after you were at our house for supper, I saw Willie carrying something long and thin into the barn. Later after he had gone to sleep, I went out to the barn to see what he had hidden in there. I finally found it up in the loft, hidden underneath all the hay."

"What was it?"

"Three branding irons were wrapped up in a blanket."

Travis slapped his thigh, "Doggone it," and everybody in the store including Miss Peet looked over to see what had happened. Ethan covered by fumbling with some pots and lids on the shelf.

"I guess you know what that means," Travis said in a quiet tone. "There's only one reason anyone not involved with ranching would have branding irons."

"Yep," said Ethan. "Cattle rustling."

"He could get into some real trouble for that."

"Could he get hanged?" Ethan asked with a look of concern.

"Not likely. But it's possible. The death penalty is more common for horse thieves than cattle rustlers. But he could go to prison for a very long time."

Ethan stopped arranging the pots. "What should I do?"

"Do you think he's dangerous? I mean would he hurt you if he knew that you were on to him?"

"Oh, no. If there's one thing I know, it's that Willie would never do anything to hurt me. He's always looked out for me."

"Well then, you've got to talk to him. Plead with him to stop what he's doing."

"I suppose I could try. I don't know if he will listen."

"That's the best you can do, and if he persists with what he's doing, it's out of your hands."

Ethan thought about the farm. If Willie went to prison, what would happen to him and his mother? Could they keep the farm going without him? He best not think about it right now.

"So what did you want to talk to me about?"

"You know I'm leaving on the cattle drive in two weeks," Travis said. He fondled the rim of his hat. Ethan glanced at his hands, then looked back up. The hat had left a flattened area of his sun-bleached hair above his forehead. "Well, how would you feel about signing onto the drive and coming with me?"

Ethan hadn't expected this, but the invitation and the manner in which Travis delivered it snagged his imagination. "Me? On a cattle drive?" He had never in a hundred years pictured himself as a cowboy herding cows.

"Sure," Travis said. "You're a great rider and you could learn the other stuff real quick. It would be a wonderful experience for you. I could show you some of this beautiful country I've been talking about. Mr. Bennet still needs a few more hands." Travis stopped fidgeting with his hat, crossed his arms, gave Ethan one of his famous grins and raised his eyebrows. "Plus, you will earn more than twice what you would make here at the store in the same three months"

"I don't know. I would have to get permission from my

mother." He was considering the money. Twice the amount he would make at the store. His mother might really need that money if Willie landed in jail, maybe it could even save the farm. Nobody ever said that taking care of her was Willie's job alone.

"Why? You're a man now. How old are you?"

"I'm seventeen."

"See. You don't need your mother's permission. Just let her know that you'll be going. She can't stop you."

Ethan thought about it for a moment. He wouldn't have to say goodbye to Travis. He could spend a lot of time with him. But the thought of him traipsing across deserts and prairies behind a herd, kicking up a bunch of dust...well, still, being with Travis for three whole months kind of outweighed the discomforts of driving cattle. And there was the money.

"Okay. I'll ask my mother about it tonight."

"Good. If you decide to come along, just stop by the ranch and I'll get you all signed up." Travis slapped him on the shoulder. "See ya later, Ethan." Travis was so elated that he put his hat back on and headed straight out the door.

"Humph," Miss Peet said.

*   *   *

Ethan didn't talk to his mother that night. He took a few days to mull it all over in his head, because he wasn't yet convinced that he really wanted to go. Finally one evening when supper was finished and all the dishes were done, and the three boarders were out for the evening, and Willie was out with his buddies doing God knows what, and Ophelia was sitting in her chair in the drawing room sewing a new dress, Ethan sat up straighter on the sofa to talk.

"Mother," he began cautiously, "I've been thinking about signing up at the Haywood Ranch to go on the cattle drive this summer."

"What!" Ophelia's face was full of horror. "Ethan, No! You're too young! It's too dangerous for a boy like you." She dropped the dress pieces and thread into the sewing basket beside her chair, because this was going to take her full attention.

"I'm seventeen. I think it's time I started getting out and doing new things, seeing new towns and country. I'm not going to stick around here forever you know." His voice grew stronger. "Ma, I would make twice as much money as the store and it would be wise for us to have some money saved up."

"I know eventually you're going to move out and get married, and hopefully live someplace nearby, but I didn't think you would be leaving so soon. What about all the danger? There are savages, and you could fall into a canyon, or get trampled in a stampede."

"You heard Travis when he was here for supper. The Indians no longer claim that territory. I'll be fine. I need to do this. I *really* want to do this."

We already know that when Ophelia has something she doesn't want to deal with, she tends to bury it inside her and ignore it. She now saw that this was something over which she would have no control, so she immediately retreated.

"Well, if you're really determined to go, then I guess I can't stop you. But I will still worry every minute you're away!"

"It'll only be three months, then I'll come back and go back to working in the store, just like before."

"You had better write me letters and mail them in every town you go through, just so I'll know you're still alive."

"I promise, Ma. I will. And please don't worry. I'll be fine."

She picked her sewing back up and continued where she had left off. So his mind was now made up and everything was more or less squared away with his mother. Of course she would worry about him, but what else was new? It was her nature to worry about everything. He decided he would drop by the ranch tomorrow after work and get signed up.

*   *   *

Ethan arrived at the ranch at six thirty the next evening. Mr. Bennet had hired on quite a few new hands for the cattle drive. Four men sat on the corral fence, entertained by a roguish young cowboy doing some impersonation of a brassy whorehouse madam. Two more men stood by the barn examining each other's six-shooters. And yet another cowpoke sat on the bench in front of the bunkhouse practicing his harmonica. Ethan hoped there would still be room. He knocked on the door to the bunkhouse and a tall young man answered the door.

"Is Travis in there?" Ethan asked. The man turned around and called out "Travis in here?" Someone hollered back, "He's in the barn with the horses!" Ethan wasn't sure if this was a joke. He thanked the man and made his way to the barn. Sure enough, Travis was in there brushing out Cleo.

Travis flashed his ever-appealing smile. "So I guess you decided to sign up?"

"Yep. It's all set."

"Great! Come on up to the ranch and I'll get you all taken care of." Travis finished currying Cleo, hung the brush on a nail, locked her in her stall, and then took Ethan up to the ranch house and into Mr. Bennet's office.

"Ethan here would like to sign up for the cattle drive," Travis said to Mr. Bennet.

"Really?" Mr. Bennet raised his eyebrows. "Well, it's hard to believe you're all grown up now, Ethan. How old are you son?"

"Seventeen."

"Well, I know you're a good rider and you seem healthy and strong enough. I see no reason why you can't sign on. Is your ma okay with it?"

"She said it's fine."

"Well then all we need is your signature here." He pulled a roster out of the desk drawer. "We will supply you with a horse and gear, a bedroll and tent. You will be paid twenty-five dollars now and the remaining seventy-five at the end of the drive. After that you'll hafta turn in your horse and gear and make your way back home on your own."

Ethan didn't realize that the whole troupe wouldn't be returning together, and must have looked a little perplexed.

"Don't worry about that," Travis said. "I'll see that you get home okay."

"So, do you agree to the terms?" Mr. Bennet asked. Ethan nodded. Mr. Bennet showed him where to sign on the roster, and then paid him out twenty-five dollars.

"We leave on the first of June," Mr. Bennet said. "Be here at six a.m. sharp ready to go. We will see you then."

Chapter Seven

A week before Ethan was to leave on the cattle drive, he had taken care of most of the preparations. Mr. Simpson knew that he was quitting his job for the summer, and disapproved; he'd have to find a new boy. Travis joined Ethan at the store shortly before closing time to help him pick out some items he would need for the drive. He helped Ethan pick out a good quality canteen, a sturdy rope, some neckerchiefs, and finally a hat. A real cowboy hat was absolutely essential in the desert. Mr. Simpson carried a very limited selection of them on a shelf at the back of the store, and for the first time, Ethan looked at them carefully. He had had his eye on a tan one that made him look older. Travis agreed that Ethan could pass for at least twenty-one, under its brim, so they found one that fit well on his narrow head and arranged for Mr. Simpson to deduct the cost from his final pay. They left the store together and strolled down the street, Travis holding Cleo's reins as she trailed behind them.

"Have you talked to your brother yet?"

"Not yet."

"Well, I've got some bad news for you, Ethan. During the round-up we've found that quite a few head are missing. I'm afraid it may be your brother and his friends who are responsible."

Ethan cringed. "I'll warn him the first chance I get."

Travis hopped up on Cleo. "Take care, kid. The hat looks good."

They parted ways – Travis to the Haywood Ranch, Ethan to Miss Peet's house. Telling Miss Peet he was leaving would be easy, unlike the task he was avoiding – confronting Willie about the cattle rustling. He could feel his new responsibility sitting on him like, well, his hat. If he failed to persuade Willie to end this rustling, it might be up to him alone to provide for his mother. The drive was the right thing to do.

When he arrived at Miss Peet's house, he put on the hat, bowed his head so the brim covered his face, knocked on the door, then put his thumbs in his pockets and gave his best imitation of a cowpoke. Ethan stood there for a long time, and was beginning to think maybe she wasn't at home. Finally she opened the door.

Ethan slowly raised his head, gave a little swagger and said, "Howdy there, ma'am."

Miss Peet reeled back in surprise then began to laugh. "Ethan! Oh that's so funny! Why are you pretending to be a cowboy?"

He came inside. It was obvious that she was not expecting company. There were school papers strewn all over the dining room table. She had no tea, no lemonade, and no coffee, and apologized up and down for her inability to be a better hostess.

"Why on earth are you wearing a cowboy hat?"

"I've decided to go on the cattle drive to Cheyenne," he answered.

She burst out laughing. "Oh Ethan, but seriously!"

"I'm not joking. I'm all signed up. I'm leaving in a week."

Her laughter subsided and her face grew concerned. "But why? In all the years I've known you, you never showed an inkling of interest in being a cowpoke."

"I never was interested, until now."

"I just don't understand. What brought this on?"

"I decided I wanted adventure. To see the country. To do something different for a change."

"That's not at all what I envisioned you doing with your life.

Punching cows. You're too smart for that. I always thought you would go to college and become a respectable businessman." Her face hardened. "Have you thought about the dangers? With all the savage Indians around, you could be killed!"

"Now you're starting to sound just like my mother."

"Well, you *were* my pupil. And I feel a maternal responsibility toward all my pupils."

"I'm not choosing to be a cowboy for life, just for the summer. Then I'll come back and work in the store again."

Her face softened again and a smile broke through. "Well, in that case maybe it's not the greatest tragedy since Romeo and Juliet. Let me see you in that hat again."

He put the hat on, got up and swaggered around the room doing his best impersonation of a cowboy. Miss Peet giggled, then Ethan started laughing.

When Miss Peet finally managed to regain her composure, she said, "Well, you do make a very handsome cowboy."

This sent Ethan back into a whole new fit.

"I just realized something," Miss Peet said. "Travis will be with you on the cattle drive! This would be the perfect opportunity for you to plant a little seed of romance in his head."

"I beg your pardon?"

"I mean, you can warm him up to the idea of courting me."

"Oh. I don't know. I'm not really much for matchmaking."

"You don't have to say much. Just give him a little prod."

Ethan removed the hat and began curling the edges. "You know what's funny about the cattle drive? I can only bring two or three sets of clothes. Generally cowboys only have two sets, one that they're wearing and one that they're washing. There's no room to bring a whole wardrobe."

Her smile faded and she cocked her head. "That's interesting. What about books? Is there room to take books? You will need a diversion of some sort."

"That's what I thought," Ethan answered. "But Travis laughed at me when I told him I wanted to bring some books. It makes no sense to him why anybody would want to read when they are out taking in all the beautiful country. He told me that I would be working so hard that by the end of the day, after a hot meal, I would be so exhausted I would be asleep as soon as my eyes closed. Some of the vaqueros carry a journal to write in, but that's it."

"I'm going to miss your visits," Miss Peet said all of a sudden, eyes wet. "But you'll have so much to tell me when you get back."

*   *   *

A few days before the cattle drive, Willie was out back chopping wood for the stove. The air was still, and a quiet desolation hovered over the fields. They were bumpy with tan dirt and rock, cluttered with patches of dry sagebrush. Split timbers were neatly stacked five feet high against the back wall of the house. A few remaining logs lay beside the chopping block, a battered stump. The setting sun bathed Willie and the tree stump in an orange glow. Ethan stood at the corner of the house, leaning with his hand against the side. Willie's skillful, forceful swings were splitting the logs with single blows. Ethan thought back to when Willie was the twelve year old boy eager to go hunting with his father, trailing after him and doting on the guns. Now, Willie's black curls stuck to his forehead with perspiration, and Ethan realized for the first time that his brother was actually a full-grown man. He took a deep breath, walked up to the tree stump, and faced Willie.

"Willie," he said. "I know what's been going on."

The axe was poised to fall, but Willie gently stopped mid-swing and lowered it to the ground. "What on earth are you talking about, little brother?"

"I know what you and Jim and Horace have been doing."

"Some gambling? Bit of drinking? Whores? Nothing you haven't done."

"I know you guys have been cattle rustling."

"I don't know who you been talking to, brother, but how dare you accuse me of that?"

Ethan shifted his weight from one foot to the other, his eyes focused on the half-split log. His voice was low and calm. "Willie, I've seen the branding irons."

Willie turned white as a Lipizzaner stallion. He dropped the handle of the axe, looked around, and drew in close to Ethan.

"You're not going to turn us in are you?"

"Of course not. But you've got to stop. Get rid of those branding irons and never do it again."

Willie's eyes were wide, his face reverting back to the jaded gambler. "Oh I will, little brother. I will. I promise!"

"Because if you got caught and went to jail, mother would go out of her mind. You've got to think about that."

Willie stumbled over himself to reach out, seize his brother's hand and shake it heartily, looking a bit of a fool. "I give you my word, Ethan. It's over."

Ethan still wasn't sure about that, so before work the next morning, he went into the barn and checked the loft. The branding irons were gone, but in the back of his mind he wondered if Willie hadn't just found a better hiding place.

*　　*　　*

The night of May 31st, Ethan lay awake in bed. His boots and chaps were clean and his spurs polished. Folded on his bureau were two clean shirts, two pairs of trousers, his undergarments, and his hat. He was all set to be up at five-thirty and be off.

His goodbyes had been taken care of earlier in the evening. His mother had prepared a special farewell dinner of roast tenderloin steak, and everyone ate heartily except Ethan. Besides Mr. Baker, Mr. Pendegast, and Mr. Ponce, Miss Peet and the sheriff joined them at the table. Willie was on his best behavior. As they went around the table, offering advice to Ethan, Willie was all earnest smiles. "Take care of yourself, little brother, and don't worry, I'll keep up the farm while you're away. Everything will be fine here." It may have sounded to everyone else that he was going to take over Ethan's duties around the farm, but Ethan didn't do that much on the farm. There was another meaning to Willie's statement, which Ethan feared: that the cattle-rustling would continue. The money was very important now. He must earn this money to ensure that his mother's farm and boarding house were safe.

As he lay in bed waiting for sleep to come, he wondered what tomorrow was going to be like. He wondered what kind of horse he would be given. And what would the other vaqueros be like?

Would they be more like Travis, or just like Fred, Don and Joe? Would they pick on him for being a bookish little kid? If it weren't for the fact that Travis would be there to look out for him, he would never have agreed to go. He had only one strong premonition: He was about to embark upon the greatest adventure of his life.

The Second Part:
The Drive

Chapter One

"Ethan! Get down here and help us out!" He was riding at the rear flank of the herd, the cry came from Ethan's left side. He spotted Patrick and David down in a shallow ravine. They had cornered one of the cows. She was butted up against a crevice in the ravine wall and refused to budge. Patrick had his rope around her neck and David had his rope around her horns. They were both pulling with all their might, but she dug in her hooves and stared at them as if to say, "I'm tired and I'm not going to walk another inch for you bastards!" Ethan hopped off his horse and half-walked and half-slid down the slope to the bottom of the ravine. He got behind the cow and started pushing on her rump. It was no good. She was very large and very strong and more than a match for three tired humans.

Patrick and David had been cow punching for most of their lives. They had formed a close friendship but quarreled whenever there was trouble, and due to their equally weathered skin and stubbly cheeks, it was difficult to judge their age, let alone tell them apart. They were both lean, tall, and strong. Both had shoulder-length, curly brown hair, though David had a touch of gray in the temples. Neither was particularly intelligent, but they both knew all the ins and outs of driving cattle, and Patrick appeared to have the seniority of experience and often took the lead in these situations. You couldn't really call either of them handsome, but their ability had an attractive quality.

"Go get your rope Ethan; you can use it to whip her," Patrick shouted. Ethan climbed back out of the ravine and retrieved his rope. The herd had now completely passed them by. He scooted back down the slope and began whipping the cow on her hindquarters, until she yielded and trotted out from the crevice to get away from that stinging rope.

"Now how are we gonna get her back up the bank?" Ethan asked.

"I have an idea." Patrick (or David?) took the rope off the cow's horns and tied it to the rope around her neck in a very tight slipknot. He then climbed up the slope with the rope, which was now long enough to reach the top. He mounted his horse and tied the rope around his saddlehorn. Now the cow had no choice but climb out of the ravine, or else be dragged out by her neck. Ethan cheered. Patrick stayed behind to bring the cow in at her slower pace, and Ethan got back on his horse and galloped off to rejoin the herd. As Ethan took his place in the formation, Travis dropped back.

"Everything okay? What happened back there?"

"Just a stray. We had to pull her out of a hole. David's bringing her back in."

Travis glanced back at the other rider. "No, that's Patrick there." Travis gave him a hard pat on the back and then galloped back up to his position at the middle of the herd.

Less than an hour later, the herd reached their destination like clockwork. The sun was starting to go down. They had been on the trail for a couple of weeks now, and Mr. Bennet seemed to have a specific place that he knew about every night where they would set up camp. Bunny, the cook began building the fire for supper, half the cowboys tended to settling the herd for the night, and the other half began pitching the tents. Once the work was done, the cowboys sat around the campfire waiting for supper to be ready. They were all exhausted and this was their time to relax and unwind. Virgil took out his harmonica, leaned back, propped up his feet and began to play a mournful tune. The cowboys sat and listened staring into the fire. It was peaceful, almost hypnotic. While everyone was in this little trance, Josh came up from the river carrying a soppy shirt he had just washed. He snuck up behind Virgil and wrung the shirt out over his head, releasing a small torrent of water into his face.

"That's better, Virgil. Your music was too dry!"

Virgil jumped up and lunged at Josh. But Josh, laughing hysterically, took off with Virgil in hot pursuit. Virgil managed to catch him and tackled him.

"I oughtta wring your neck!" Instead he grabbed the wet shirt from Josh and threw it in the dirt.

"Aw, now what did you have to go and do that for? Now I gotta wash it again! Jeez, Virgil, it was only a joke."

"Yep, and now everybody's laughing." It was true. All the cowboys around the fire were well entertained. Josh picked up his shirt and trudged back down to the river.

Mr. Bennet had noticed Ethan watching the spectacle. "They're just letting off a little steam," he said. "They know what's coming up and they're a little worried."

"What's coming up?"

"In a couple of days we're going to leave the Concho River behind and cross the Llano Estacado."

"What's that?"

"Son, that's eighty miles of barren desert. It's a sonofabitch and we've got to cross it fast, or the herd will die of thirst. Before we leave the river, we'll rest the herd for a day and get them to drink as much as they can, then we'll drive them straight across the dessert without stopping."

"Whoa." Ethan was stunned. "How long will it take to cross?"

"About three days. If we take any longer, the herd will start to die. And another thing. When the herd gets thirsty, they get restless and unruly. There's a big chance of a stampede."

"Come now, Bennet," Travis interrupted. "You're scaring the kid. It's not all that bad. I've been on this trail before. It's highly unlikely we're going to have a stampede."

Mr. Bennet gave a little "Humph" and acquiesced. Despite Mr. Bennet's doom and gloom, Ethan let Travis reassure him. His stomach started grumbling. What was taking so long with supper? He looked over at the chow wagon and saw Bunny hurrying back and forth with the preparations. Bunny was an old geezer with a big round belly and scraggy gray beard. He had a round face and small crinkled eyes. He was always fussing with the cowboys and telling them to get away and leave him alone so he could do his job. His nasty disposition marked him as a target for the cowboys, and they took pleasure in getting him riled up.

After a good long wait, Bunny finally rang the supper bell and everyone grabbed their tin bowls and cups and stood in line for their stew. Ethan took his bowl of stew and hunk of stale bread and sat back down by the fire to contemplate the information he had just been given while he ate. For the first time since the drive had begun, he had an uneasy feeling. He was dreading having to cross that desert already. If it weren't for the confidence he had in Travis, he might have lost his nerve for the cattle drive right then and there.

*   *   *

"Ethan, wake up! It's time for your shift." It was Travis's voice from outside his tent flap. It seemed like he had only just closed his eyes. There were sixteen men, each stood guard over the herd for one hour each night. This meant that Ethan could get a full night's sleep every other night. This wasn't the night.

"I'm awake. What time is it?"

"Two a.m."

Ethan slipped out of his bedroll, pulled on his boots and coat, and came out of the tent. Guard duty was very easy. All you had to do was sit and watch the herd for an hour to make sure they stayed put, and no rustlers came to steal them. Since the herd was usually sleeping, there wasn't anything to do but sit and watch. He and Travis walked together to the herd and sat down on some logs. Whenever it was Ethan's shift, Travis always stayed up a few minutes to talk.

"So how was your father killed?"

Ethan looked sharply at Travis, yawned, and lowered his eyes. "All I know is it was a gunfight with another man. I don't know who it was or what the fight was about. Me and Willie used to ask our mother about it, but she said she doesn't know. I think she does, but she just doesn't want to talk about it. She's like that. Anything bad or upsetting, she just denies."

"What do you remember about when he died?"

"I was eight and Willie was twelve. One night he didn't come home from town. He was supposed to have some kind of business to take care of. I remember he was going into town for business a lot at that time. When it got really late, Ma woke us up and told us she was going into town to look for our father and we were to stay put and bolt the door behind her and wait. Well, we were waiting so long, we finally fell asleep by the fire. The next thing I remember is waking up hearing Ma pounding on the door to let her in. She was crying and she hugged us both real tight and told us our father had gone to heaven to be with Jesus. We both knew that meant he was dead. I was comforting Ma, but Willie was very angry. He wanted to know what had happened, but Ma was too upset to tell us anything.

"So once Willie found out our father had been killed in a gunfight, he vowed that someday he would get revenge by killing the man who did it."

"What about you? Were you upset by your father's death?"

"Not like Willie was. Pa really liked Willie. I just felt bad that I wasn't able to make him proud before he died. But I didn't mourn for him the way Willie did."

"You didn't think your father was proud of you?"

"He was always very proud of Willie. He took Willie fishing and hunting and taught him how to shoot a rifle. It seemed like I could never do anything right for him. I don't know why. I tried, but nothing I ever did was good enough. Finally he just gave up on me and spent all his time teaching Willie stuff. That's why Willie was so devastated when he died.

"I remember this one time, I was maybe five or six, it was my father's birthday and I told Ma I wanted to bake him a cake for his birthday. She thought it was a great idea so she helped me. Actually I know now that she really baked the cake and I just helped her, but she made me feel like I was doing it. After it was all perfect and placed in the middle of the table, I was excited and couldn't wait for my daddy to get home, so I could show it to him. When he finally got home that night, I ran up to him, hugged him and said 'Daddy, Daddy, happy birthday! Look what I made for you! I baked you a cake!' He gave me a strange look, and didn't say anything. After supper Ma cut the cake and I was anxious to have him taste it. He told Ma no thanks, he didn't want any. Ma said to him, 'Jack please, Ethan made it for your birthday.' He yelled, 'I said no!' Ma could see that my feelings were hurt, so she cut herself a big slice and ate it telling me it was the best birthday cake she had ever tasted."

"I'm sorry," Travis said. "You poor little kid. Your father was very cruel. I know you think it was important to have his approval, but you really don't need it. You know, even if he had lived, chances are he never would have given it to you, and you might have spent your whole life trying to gain it."

"Yeah." Ethan looked down at the ground. "That's probably right."

"Is your mother proud of you?"

"Yes."

"How about your schoolteacher, Miss Peet? I know she's proud of you. You see? There are plenty of people whose approval you already have. You don't need your father's."

He reached over and mussed Ethan's hair. "I'm gonna go get some sleep tonight. I'll see you in the morning."

"Good night, Travis."

"'Night, Ethan."

Chapter Two

They had arrived at the spot where they were to leave the Concho River. The herd was spending the entire day resting, grazing and drinking. It was a nice lush green area by the river and most of the men lounged around and enjoyed their day off. They had finished a big breakfast, a mighty good one of flapjacks with syrup and steak and potatoes. Since Bunny didn't have to hurry to pack everything up, he was able to take his time and make an extra special breakfast.

Ethan had nothing better to do, so he decided to take a walk up the river and see some of the countryside. As he was meandering along, throwing stones into the river and thinking about what he was going to write in his letters to his mother and Miss Peet, he spotted a pale body swimming in the river. It was Travis.

Ethan ducked behind a bush and crept closer. He got as close as he could while still keeping himself concealed. Travis was up to his waist in the river and had lathered his whole upper body with soap. His torso was nicely developed. The skin was much lighter than his hands and face, since he rarely ever took off his shirt. He had a perfect little trail of light brown hair between his pectoral muscles. Then he washed his hair and face. Ethan, peering through the bush, was very tense and scarcely moved or breathed. He had often thought about what Travis might look like naked, and now he was very likely to find out. After Travis finished scrubbing his hair, he ducked down under the water to rinse himself off. He stood back up and slicked back his hair with his hands. He then headed towards the bank. As he approached the riverbank, the water level descended on his body, and he emerged from the river. Travis stood there naked on the riverbank, smoothing the excess water from his hair. Droplets glistened in the sun and dripped off his body. His thighs were powerful and pale as his chest, and downy with fine brown hair. He dried himself off, causing his dangling genitals to bounce a bit, then pulled on his trousers and shirt.

At the moment Travis's body had been revealed, Ethan's breath shuddered, his heart pounded, and his head tingled, as if he were about to pass out. His body was paralyzed. He yearned to be able to touch, to caress; it made his fingers sweat. He wanted to be close to Travis, and more than anything to always be his friend.

Spying could end their friendship. So Ethan waited until Travis had headed back to camp and was completely out of sight, then he emerged from his hiding place and continued wandering up the river, going over and over the image in his head.

*   *   *

By the time Ethan got back to camp it was already past noon and Bunny was cooking the midday meal. Travis was brushing Cleo while he talked to Virgil. Virgil was a tall lanky cowboy in his late twenties, generally neat appearance, short hair, dark features and droopy sad eyes. He was normally kind of quiet. When he did talk, it was usually about his soon to be wife, who was waiting for him in Cheyenne. After the cattle drive, they were to be married.

Travis smiled as Ethan walked up to them. "Good afternoon, Ethan. What you been up to?"

"Just out exploring."

Travis nodded and then went back to his discussion with Virgil. "So are you going to continue cow punchin' after you're married?"

"Naw, my Betsy won't stand for that. She can't have me gone for long periods of time, and I would worry about her being alone for so long too. I'm gonna see If I can get a job working for the blacksmith in Laramie."

"Laramie?"

"Yeah. That's where her folks live and that's where we're gonna live too."

"Very nice. Do you have a house there?"

"Not yet. We're gonna live with her folks for awhile until we can get ourselves situated into our own place."

"Good. Laramie's nice country. I wouldn't mind living there myself. Although personally, I think I would rather live in Colorado. It's got the most beautiful land in the country."

"Yeah. I've heard that. But Betsy's got to be near her family. They mean a lot to her."

Travis turned to Ethan. "Are you ready for tomorrow? We've got to start out early. So get lots of sleep tonight, because you're not going to be sleeping much for the next three days."

Ethan nodded, "I'll be ready." Bunny was ringing the dinner bell now, so the three cowboys ambled over to join the rest of the company for dinner.

*   *   *

The entire camp was up well before dawn. Travis and Ethan had already packed their bedrolls and tents and were ready to go by the time the rest of the men were still drinking their coffee, so the two of them went down to the river to watch the sun come up.

"I love this time of the morning," Travis said. "I don't know why, but it's like the sounds are more vivid. The rushing water, the crickets and frogs. Even the wind. You can hear everything, no matter how far away it is. After the sun comes up, it's like the heat deadens everything."

"I never really thought about it before. But I guess I can hear stuff now that I don't remember hearing during the day."

Waiting for the sunrise, they listened to the soft gurgle of water cascading over the rocks, the faraway song of a whippoorwill, the clanging of pots and pans as Bunny packed the wagon back at camp.

"You ever been with a woman, Ethan?"

Why did Travis do that? Ethan blushed. With any other guy he knew that he would have to lie to avoid being ridiculed. He

77

picked up a twig and scraped in the crevice of a rock.

"No."

"I didn't think so."

"How about you? Have you…been, with a woman?"

"Yes. I've been with a few."

"Were you in love with them?"

"No, I can't say that. It had very little to do with love." Travis had a distant look in his face, almost like he was thinking of something else. "Do you think you'll ever get married someday, Ethan?"

Ethan recalled the image he often had of himself in black tie and tails at his small church wedding. "I suppose so. How about you?"

"I intend to share my life with someone, but to be married in the traditional sense? No, I won't do that. I do intend to share my life with someone I love."

"These women you were with. How did you know them?"

"Well, the first one was a girl I knew from childhood. She was sweet on me and we were good friends. When we became of age, she kind of had the idea we were going to be married. We even went so far as to sleep together, but I knew she wasn't going to be the one. So when I refused to propose, she got mad and said she never wanted to see me again. I think she was upset because in her mind she had sacrificed her virginity for nothing."

"What was her name?"

"I'm sorry, Ethan. I can't tell you that. I feel that I owe her the respect of keeping it secret that we were together. I could never let out information that could harm her reputation."

Ethan nodded. "That's fair. What about the others?"

"They were mostly girls I met in towns where I was working as a ranch hand. I would respond to their flirting and go to bed with them, hoping that one of them would feel right and be the one who would be everything for me. Some of them just wanted a good time, and some of them wanted a husband. None of them moved me to love them."

Ethan was intrigued. He knew that most men slept with whores before they got married. But he had never heard of women sleeping around and not getting paid for it.

"So do you think you will ever find this perfect girl?"

Travis looked right into Ethan's eyes. "I have no doubt." He tossed a stone into the river rapids, now glimmering golden in the sunrise.

Chapter Three

The dreaded Llano Estacado. Thirty-seven thousand square miles of arid, windswept, treeless plateau. Gently inclining upwards to the northeast, it is encompassed by the Canadian River at the north, the Pecos River at the west, and the precipitous cliffs of the Caprock Escarpment at the east. It covers most of the land around the Texas and New Mexico border. Its name means The Staked Plains. It is believed that American Indians and Spanish explorers, finding no landmarks in the vast desert, drove stakes in the ground to mark their trails. This particular journey would only traverse its smallest corner.

Ethan's place was with Josh at the rear of the herd. In the Llano Estacado, that was the worst place to be. The herd kicked up so much dust that Ethan and Josh covered their mouths and noses with bandanas, and by midday they were filthy. The heat rebounded off the desert floor. They only stopped every two or three hours to rest and water the horses. The midday and evening meals were prepared quickly and served cold, Mr. Bennet was so determined to keep the herd moving at a steady pace.

By mid-afternoon of the first day Ethan was worn out and parched. If he was this exhausted, he couldn't imagine how the poor cows felt. They were doing it with no water at all. The sun went down and still they kept going – the first time they had traveled at night. A quarter moon provided sufficient light between the dust clouds. He leaned back in his saddle under the myriad of stars in the sky.

As the night wore on, Josh started to slump in his saddle. His head would bob and then snap back to attention. At nineteen, he was the second-youngest cowboy on the drive. He was short, about five-four, and had a bulldog's build. His short blond hair tended to bristle up when he took off his hat. And yet he had the most cheerful personality of the whole group, and was the one who clowned with the other guys, blue eyes twinkling with delight. He boasted and chattered about anything. The guys liked having him around.

Josh fell asleep and proceeded to fall off his horse. Ethan stifled a laugh and guided his own horse over to where Josh was sitting on the ground, stunned.

"You okay?"

"Yeah. I'm fine. What happened?"

"You fell asleep on your horse."

He stood up and dusted off his pants. "Ethan, do me a favor and don't tell the other guys about this, okay?"

He planned on telling Travis about it for a good laugh, but he said, "Of course I won't."

Josh hopped back up on his horse and rode beside Ethan for a while to keep himself awake.

"Have you ever been on this trail before?"

"Nope. It's my first drive, ever," said Ethan.

"Do you have any idea what the next town is?"

"Nope."

"I wonder how far it is. I'll have to ask some of the other guys. You know what I want to do when I get to the next town?"

"What?"

"First, I'm gonna get a shave. These whiskers are starting to itch me something fierce."

The rest of the men, including Josh, had already grown full-fledged beards. Ethan only had a few scraggily little whiskers on his own chin.

"Then you know what I'm gonna do? I'm gonna find the whorehouse. I hope it's one of those nice ones. You know the kind where you can take a hot bath? Then I'm gonna go get some beer. That's what I need. A shave, a bath, a whore and some beer. How about you? What are you gonna do, Ethan?"

"That all sounds pretty good." All except for the whore. Ethan still wasn't quite ready for a whore. He rode on in silence listening to Josh chatter on endlessly about mostly nothing.

*   *   *

The next day and night were uneventful. By now, Ethan's body had adjusted to the lack of sleep. He had gotten his second wind or else was numb to the exhaustion. The Llano Estacado was just a boring, endless trek. Travis would occasionally drop back to the rear of the herd to ask Ethan how he was holding up, and they'd swap news.

"Bennet's been spitting nails," Travis said.

"Why? What's wrong?"

"We're not making good pace. The herd has been too sluggish. He thinks we're not going to make it without losing some cows. Like I said, I've been on this trail before, and once it even took four whole days and we didn't lose one. It'll be fine. You'll see. Bennet just needs to listen to me and calm down."

By the third day, Mr. Bennet forbid them from even stopping for meals. Whenever they got hungry, they would just ride up beside the supply wagon and Bunny would hand over some jerky and bread. The herd was so frantic with thirst it began to get unruly. Small factions of cows began to break off from the herd, and the cowboys had to work extra hard to bring them back in. Just as the sun was at its most intense on the afternoon of the third day, the cows at the rear of the herd, mad with thirst and exhaustion, began to revolt and disperse out to the sides. Ethan tried to round them up, but they were starting to stampede. They curved around and started charging right towards Ethan. His horse spooked, reared up and fell on its side as the cows swarmed around. The pain was the most intense Ethan had ever felt in his life. The horse was lying on top of his leg and it felt like he had been stabbed with a knife. The cows had now stopped running and were scattered all about. Josh had seen the whole thing, and galloped up to where Ethan and his horse lay. He jumped down and was quickly by Ethan's side. He freed Ethan's foot from the stirrup and pulled on the bridle to coax the horse to get up. The horse rose up off Ethan's leg and Josh knelt down to examine him. He moved Ethan's leg so he could see the other side. A sharp rock had gashed it wide open. It had cut right through his chaps and pants and cut open the skin, and the wound filled with blood.

"Jesus Christ, Your leg!"

Ethan was faint from the pain. "What is it?"

"It's hurt bad. I'll be right back." Josh swung himself onto his horse and galloped off for help.

Maybe they would have to leave him behind in order to save the cows. Mr. Bennet was sure to be riled about this. He could imagine what his mother and Miss Peet would say: See? Didn't we *warn* you about the dangers?

Travis was the first one at Ethan's side, and already had his knife in his hand. He removed Ethan's chaps, and cut Ethan's pant leg open the rest of the way.

His face obscured by the brim of his hat, Travis spoke quickly, his words forced. "It's not that bad, Ethan. You're gonna be just fine. We'll get you all patched up."

Mr. Bennet arrived with Josh. He took one look at the leg and said, "It's not too serious. Hurry and get him bandaged up, Travis. We've got to get this herd rounded up and back on the trail!"

Bunny pulled up in the supply wagon. Travis and Josh lifted Ethan up and sat him down in the wagon. Mr. Bennet headed off to organize the round-up and Travis proceeded to wash out the gash in Ethan's thigh. There was a lot of dirt and it took about ten ladles of water and some serious swabbing to get it all washed out. He took a bottle of alcohol, warned Ethan it was going to hurt, and poured it into the wound. He then took long bandage strips and bound the thigh. He took a bedroll, rolled it out onto the floor of the wagon and eased Ethan down onto it.

"You just lay there and rest until you're feeling better."

"But what about... the cows? Are they..."

"Don't worry. We can handle it. You just rest." Travis closed the wagon gate and tied Ethan's horse to the back of the wagon and went to join in the round-up.

In a short time Ethan felt the wagon begin to roll bumpily

underneath him. The loss of blood and the lack of sleep caught up to him, and not even the bumps in the terrain could keep him from falling asleep.

*   *   *

Ethan woke up to the sound of Travis's voice. It felt like the middle of the night.

"Did we make it to the river, Travis?"

"Not yet. Are you feeling better?"

Ethan sat up. A dull pain throbbed in his leg. He tried moving his foot but all the muscles had stiffened up during his sleep.

"I guess I'm a little better."

"The cows are getting restless and we could use your help. Do you think you can ride yet?"

"Yeah. I can do it." Ethan slowly got down out of the wagon and tried walking. He limped severely, but limping was walking. He put on his cut-up chaps, which held his sliced-open pant leg in place over his bandages. Travis gave him a boost up onto his horse, and he took his place back at the rear of the herd.

Josh brought his horse up alongside. "Hey partner, I ain't ever seen so much blood!"

The herd started moving again and the riders pushed it on through the night. In the coolness, the cows were a little less feisty and there were no more incidents that night.

Just as the faint glow of dawn began to emanate from the horizon, Josh dropped back next to Ethan. His face showed concern – he frowned and bit his lower lip. Ethan didn't have to ask.

"You know it's been three whole days, Ethan."

"Yeah, I know."

"The guys are sayin' that if you don't make it in three days, you don't make it."

Ethan didn't respond. He didn't have an answer.

"You think we're close to the river now?"

"I don't know. I hope."

"The cows won't make it through another day of all that heat and no water. I talked to some of the other guys who've done this drive before, and they're all real grumpy-like. It makes me a little scared."

"Well, we may lose a few cows. I'm sure that's all it is."

"Yeah, but what if we lose the whole herd? They don't pay nothin' for dead cows rotting in the desert."

"Then I guess we won't get paid." Ethan was being a little matter-of-fact, but he truly didn't know what to say. Josh was looking for encouragement and Ethan didn't have any to spare. The eastern horizon glowed a pale yellow. Ethan and a somber Josh rode on in silence until Travis dropped back to check on Ethan.

"How's your leg feel?"

The wound throbbed, but riding didn't hurt it any more. "A little better."

"Good. The herd's quieted down a bit, so you should be able to take it pretty easy. Hey Josh, why the long face?"

"It's been three days already."

"So it has. And today we're going to reach the Pecos and it will all be over."

Josh was frowning. "Are you sure about that, Travis?"

"We may be cutting it a little close this time, but we'll make it. There's nothing to worry about. Now come on, buck up and show me the Josh we're all used to. Think about something else. Start planning how you're going to spend all that money once the drive is over!"

Josh smiled. The first rays of sun shot like bright bullets over the horizon, Josh bounded off to the other side of the herd with a fresher spirit. Travis stayed behind.

"We're really going to make it okay, Travis?"

Travis dropped his eyes. He was obviously going to be a little more honest with Ethan than he had been with Josh. "We'll make it okay, but I'm afraid we just may lose a few cows."

"How many? A whole lot?"

"No, not a lot. But I hate to lose any, and by God, we won't if I can help it." Travis tightened his grip on the reins and sat up straighter. "I'm glad your leg is better; you gave me a good scare back there. Your mother and Miss Peet would never have forgiven me if I'd let something happen to you." Travis grinned and clicked at his horse, and galloped ahead, out of sight.

Exercise loosened up the stiffness in Ethan's leg and the pain barely registered. Or maybe he had just acclimated to the pain, but either way he felt much better.

The sun reached its zenith, and the overheated, exhausted and completely dehydrated cows began to slow down. The desert stretched endlessly before them, and they had reached their breaking point. Some of them staggered and fell. Whenever that happened, one or two of the cowboys whipped her back up and onward. It seemed merciless, driving creatures so hard to an inevitable death, but Mr. Bennet was desperate. He rode around the circumference of the herd shouting, "Keep 'em going boys! We're almost there! Keep those cows moving!" But still the herd faltered. The river was nowhere in sight. Ethan couldn't see how it was possible. Two stumbling cows finally collapsed and refused to get back up. Patrick and David started whipping them. The herd moved on and left them behind, but still they whipped. Travis saw what they were doing and he bounded back to the fallen creatures. He hated to see animals mistreated. Even cows.

"You guys go on and take your places. I'll take care of this," he said. They looked perplexed but did as they were ordered.

Travis caught up to the supply wagon.

"Whoa, Bunny! Turn this thing around! I need you to go back!"

"Are you crazy? Why you want me to go back?"

"JUST DO IT, GODDAMIT! NOW!"

"Okay, but Mr. Bennet's not gonna like this!"

"You let me worry about Mr. Bennet. He can't complain about me saving two of his precious cows!"

Travis led the wagon back to where they lay. All this time Ethan had been sitting on his horse observing the scene. Now he headed over to help. Travis took the horse trough out of the wagon and set it in front of the cows. He poured water out of the last barrel, leaving but a few ladles' worth. The cows slowly drank the water and began to revive. They were soon on their feet and Ethan and Travis tied their ropes around each of the cows and began to lead them back. The herd had slowed down so much that it didn't take long for them to catch up. The two cows rejoined the herd and were as good as new.

The herd plodded slower and slower. There just didn't seem to be any point in trying to push it when it had nothing left to give. Ethan felt for sure that any minute now more cows would start to drop. And there was no water left to revive them this time. Still they rode on, the pace slackening all the way. Ethan was covered in dust. His canteen only had a few swallows left. As he looked out over the desert plain, the landscape rippled. The heat was taunting him. The cowboys all rode along silently with their heads hung low. Then suddenly through the quiet treading of the cows Ethan heard a shout. Then another. The news made it all the way to the back of the herd. The Pecos. They were going to make it. Even the cows sensed the news and quickened their pace. They trudged along for another hour and at about four o'clock in the afternoon they reached the shining water. The cows and horses all began to glut themselves on it, and all the cowboys, except for Ethan and Travis, whooped and hollered and jumped into the river fully clothed.

Chapter Four

The next few days were leisurely. Where they once had been traveling twenty to twenty-five miles a day, they only managed half that, following the course the Pecos set northward. The wounds that the Llano Estacado had left on their souls were healing, unlike the scar that was blazed on Ethan's thigh.

Ever since watching Travis bathe, Ethan had a growing appetite to see it again. He looked for opportunities to spy on Travis, but because he dreaded getting caught, found none.

One evening after supper, the whole troupe was seated around the campfire except for a few of the older men who had turned in for the night.

"I once saw the most beautiful woman," Josh said while gazing into the fire. Most of the others looked up. "I had heard the guys around town talking about this girl who would sit out on her porch every evening. They said she was very, very beautiful. The only thing was that she lived in a house that was forty miles away from town. So I decided one day I was going to go and see her for myself. And I did."

"You rode forty miles? Just to see a girl?" Fred asked.

"Yep. It took me all day to get there. But I did."

Some of the guys snickered, but most were impressed at Josh's determination.

"When I finally got there that evening, sure enough, there she sat, pretty as a picture. And I don't mean pretty like a whore, I mean she was a beautiful *lady*. I rode by very slowly and tipped my hat. She nodded back at me. She was sitting in a rocking chair doing something with a needle and yarn."

"Knitting?" Patrick asked.

"I don't think so. There was only one needle and it was kind of big."

"She was probably crocheting," Ethan offered.

"Probably. Whatever it was, I got a real good look at her. She had this pure milky white skin, and beautiful hazel eyes. And full red lips. And her hair was light brown and she had curls down to her shoulders. She was wearing a real pretty blue dress with short sleeves, because it was warm out, and she had smooth white arms. Her dress had frilly lace around the neck and a big bow tied in back."

The cowboys all sat pensively staring into the fire, obviously conjuring up this image for themselves.

"Wait a minute!" Fred said. "What did you say about her dress?"

"What?"

"You said she had a bow in the back of her dress. Well, how could you see that if she was sitting in a rocking chair? You're making all this up! You never saw no girl!"

The guys all groaned like they had just been duped.

"No. It's true! I really did see this girl!"

"Then how could you see the bow?"

"Well…maybe I thought about her so much afterwards I just kind of filled in some of the details in my mind. But I really did see her and she was the most beautiful woman I ever saw."

Fred backed down, "Okay, so what did you do next?"

"Nothing really. After I passed by her house, I made a big wide circle around, so she wouldn't see me coming back and I rode back to town."

"That's it?" Joe chided. "You didn't even speak to her?"

"No. But someday maybe I will. I'll go back someday, and ask her father if I can court her." There was a small chuckle from the cowboys.

"Sure, Josh," Joe said sarcastically. "A girl like that would really want to court the likes of you!"

"Why not? It could happen." More chuckles from the cowboys.

Travis, who had been quietly listening, pushed his hat back on his brow. "Don't listen to them, Josh. I've known lots of pretty women who marry guys just like you. This lady would probably be delighted to court you."

"You know what Josh?" Fred baited. "I'll bet when she opens that pretty mouth of her's, she ain't got no front teeth! And when she speaks, I'll bet she squawks just like a shrew!"

"And she probably ain't got no manners and farts in public!" Joe added.

"Stop it!" Josh pleaded. "You're ruining my image of her! I know she's beautiful and refined and a finer woman than the two of you will ever see in your lives!"

David took pity on Josh and said, over top of their laughter, "So Virgil, you're going to be getting married pretty soon. Why don't you tell us what your girl looks like?"

"No, sir!" Virgil said, "I'll not have you guys all picturing my beloved in your heads so you can drool over her. She's a refined lady and don't any of you go having thoughts about her. She'll be waiting for me in Cheyenne and you'll all see her then. But I warn you guys! Don't be a lookin' at her the way you've been talking about these other women. She's my fiancé and I won't have her gawked at!"

"Relax, Virgil," David said, "I'm sorry then. Forget I asked."

They all sat quietly staring into the fire tossing more twigs and branches into it to keep it going. After awhile Patrick (or was that David?) said, "I once saw a beautiful lady. I was on one of them river boats on the Mississippi River. Any of you ever been on a river boat?" They all shook their heads.

"I was traveling down to New Orleans to visit some of my family. So I was on this river boat, the kind with the big round paddle that spins in the back. It's real fancy inside those river boats. The rooms are like hotel rooms and there's a dining room and a room just for gambling. Can't you imagine that? They have a gambling hall right there on the boat! I must say it cost a pretty penny for the fare…"

"The girl, Patrick. Tell us about the girl!" Fred pleaded.

"Oh, yeah. Well, she was real sophisticated. She had one of them fancy dresses with a hoop skirt and it was real low cut, so that her shoulders were bare and you could even see the tops of her tits. You know, you could see the crease between her tits."

Travis sighed. "That's called cleavage."

"Yeah. And she had her hair all done up on top of her head real pretty like, and she was wearing this expensive necklace with jewels and she had dangly earrings and long white gloves. I think she must have been very rich."

"What was she doing there? I mean, on the boat?" Josh asked.

"I guess she was there to gamble. She didn't have an escort and she spent most of the time playing poker with the men."

"Wow. A woman playing poker?" David asked. "Did she win?"

"She won us blind. I think maybe we were paying more attention to her tits than to our cards."

The conversation continued on for a while, mostly about women and poker and guns. One by one the cowboys made their way to their tents for the night until only Ethan and Travis were left by the fire. Ethan leaned back to look at the night sky. The embers floated upwards, and looked like shooting stars. The only sounds were the crackle of the fire and the chirps of crickets. Ethan thought about the conversation between Travis and Virgil a week earlier.

"You said you wanted to live in Colorado someday?"

"That's right. I'd like to build a ranch there and raise horses." He sat with his boot hitched up on his knee and absent-mindedly twirled his spur. "I know exactly how I want it to be. I want a not-too-big ranch house with a porch that goes all the way around the front and sides. I want to build it on a hillside with the mountains behind it and a valley with a river in the front. And lots of trees all around. I even know what color I want to paint the house – brown.

"I'll have acres and acres of property all fenced off with plenty of room for the horses to run. And wooden fences. None of that barbed wire stuff. And a nice big roomy barn for the horses to sleep in. What do you think, Ethan?"

"It sounds like the most wonderful place in the world." He had never thought much about his own future or where he might go or what he might do once he left home. He had never even tried to have a dream. "But to live in Colorado would mean leaving your family. Won't you miss them?"

"I suppose I will miss them some. But they understand. My father didn't at first. He always expected me to take over the family business."

"What business?"

"He has a carpentry shop which belonged to my grandfather. He builds some furniture. But mostly he builds barrels and crates and stuff like that. He wanted to train me in the trade, but I wasn't interested in working indoors. I wanted to be outside, working with nature. He was disappointed, but eventually came to accept it. My mother, on the other hand, always knew I would need to go and live a different life and she even encouraged me to do so. A lot of who I am was probably influenced by her. I was only a year older than you are now when I left home and started working as a ranch hand."

"And how old are you now?" Ethan had always wondered but never asked.

"Twenty-two."

"That's about what I guessed."

"You know what's really strange though, Ethan? It's kind of hard to explain, but I feel like I live in a time and place where I don't belong. It's like I was born in the wrong era. I know that sounds really strange but do you know what I'm talking about?"

"I guess so."

"That's pretty much the reason I want to go to Colorado, so I can get away from all these people that I don't fit with. I feel much more comfortable out in the country; sort of one on one with nature. There are things about me that even my family doesn't know, or for that matter could even possibly understand."

"What kind of things?"

"All in good time Ethan, I'll tell you all in good time." Travis stoked the fire with a twig. "I do hate to leave my mother though. I feel bad for her because I know my dad doesn't treat her well. He's got a very hot temper and he can be hurtful even though he doesn't mean to be. But my mother thinks only of the welfare of others. I think that's why she wants me to get away. And she wants to find good husbands for my sisters, even though that means leaving her alone with my dad who doesn't treat her right."

Travis tossed a few handfuls of twigs onto the fire, it blazed back to life and Ethan moved his hands closer to the flames.

"How's your leg feeling?"

"It's healing up. It's not bleeding anymore and the scabs are drying out. It's starting to itch."

"You glad you came along? Or would you rather be back at home reading your books?"

"I'm really glad I came. I was a little scared in the desert, but I'm having a good time now. Since my other pants got ripped I only have one pair to wear now."

"We should be coming up to the next town in about a week. We can find a seamstress in town who can sew your pants up good as new. And we'll have to buy you some new chaps too." He chuckled, pointing at the jagged gash. "Those are pretty much ruined."

Chapter Five

"Whatcha gonna do with your money?" Josh asked as the afternoon sun blazed on the surrounding rocks and hills. The cows ahead were sluggish but stayed in formation.

"I've been saving my money for a long time to buy something very special."

Josh rode close. "Then tell me, what is it?"

Ethan's hand drifted down to his horse's mane. "I'm going to buy a filly."

"You haven't ever had a horse before?"

"Nope. It'll be my first."

"Well, why not a colt?"

"It used to not matter to me which it was, but after I rode Travis's horse Cleo, I decided I wanted a mare like his, and I want to raise her from the time she is weaned from her mother. That's why it's got to be a filly."

"You know what I'm gonna do with my money?"

"Spend it all on whores?" The remark escaped before he even realized what he was saying.

"Oh man! That's heartless! No, I'm not gonna spend *all* of it on whores! I'm gonna spend it on acting lessons."

"What?" Ethan couldn't have been more surprised than if Josh had said he was going to buy a piece of the moon. "Why do you need acting lessons?"

"Because I want to move to New York and be a stage actor. Have you ever seen a play, Ethan?"

"No."

"Well, I've seen several. And let me tell you, it's like magic. A whole new world opens up before you. You totally lose yourself in other people's lives."

"Yeah, it's just like reading books."

"No, it's different. With books it's all what you picture in your head, with plays it's actually happening right in front of your eyes. It's becomes real. So I'm going to learn how to act, then move to New York and become a great actor on the stage."

Ethan didn't know what to make of his declaration. It was completely opposite of anything he had ever imagined Josh would care about.

"Have you ever been to New York before?" Ethan asked but before Josh could answer, they came upon Patrick and David rolling around on the ground trying to kill each other. The tussle was vicious and almost anonymous. Both Ethan and Josh began yelling "Fight! Fight!" to call the rest of the cowboys back. Josh whistled to get their attention. Mr. Bennet, Virgil, and Fred showed up in a hurry and swung down to the ground. Virgil grabbed one man, and Fred grabbed the other. They pulled them apart and held them back until their tempers started to cool.

"Now what's this all about?" Mr. Bennet demanded.

"David done it. It's all his fault." Patrick replied in a slightly slurred voice. "He kept ridin' his horse too close and kickin' up dirt in my face. I asked him not to ride so close and he told me if I didn't like it, *I should move over!* Then I warned him he better move or else, and you know what he said to me then? He told me I could just *suck his cock!* Well that done it, so I knocked him off his horse! And who could blame me?"

"All right, all right. Hand 'em over boys." Mr. Bennet said holding out his hand. They each pulled a flask out of their jacket pockets and handed them to Mr. Bennet.

"Now I don't mind anyone takin' a nip now and then on the job. After all, it's hard work and we all need it, but I'll not have drunkenness while on duty. I've got a herd to get to market and I don't need to be slowed down by having my cowhands beating each other senseless." He mounted his horse and turned to leave. "Now get these two back up on their horses and let's get moving!"

*   *   *

Just as Travis had predicted, they arrived in town a week later. They rode in around noon, eager for some relaxation and amusement.   Mr. Bennet warned that they would only be spending one day in town, and would leave the next morning. The herd was kept on the outskirts of town and two cowboys at a time were to stay and guard it in two hour shifts.   Travis and Ethan volunteered for the first shift. This meant they could enjoy an uninterrupted respite. As for the rest of the cowboys, they all streamed into town, and then split up, some going directly to the whorehouse, some to the general store, some to the barber, some to the restaurants, and for those that had built up a powerful thirst – the saloon.

When they were relieved from their shift, Travis and Ethan went directly to the hotel. They were greeted at the front desk by a portly bald-headed gentleman in a starched red jacket and cuffs. He was most polite and businesslike and spoke with a forced European accent.

"Good day gentlemen. Would you like some rooms?"

"Yes.   Actually Mr. Keller and I will be sharing a single room."

"Yes. Indeed. Would both of you kindly sign the register?"

"Oh. And could you please draw some hot baths for us?"

"Absolutely, Mr. Cain," he answered, reading the name off the register. "Here is your key, if you would like to take your things upstairs, we will draw your baths straight away. When you're ready, the bathing room is located at the door just to the right of the staircase."

They picked up their saddles and gear and trudged up the staircase with spurs jangling, where they deposited their gear into the room with the number that was carved into the wood plaque attached to the key, and headed for the bathing room carrying clean clothes. There were three bathtubs inside, all separated by partitions for privacy. Two of the tubs had been filled with hot water and soap suds. Steam gently rose up and the soap had a

96

flowery scent. The floorboards were damp and the air tasted of minerals. They each went behind a partition and undressed. As Ethan dropped his dusty clothes onto the floor he suddenly became self-conscious. He wanted to peek around the partition. The thought of seeing Travis's unclothed body so near gave him goosebumps. He knew he would never get away with it, and stepped into the tub. He slowly submerged himself into the water, and the soothing, sudsy warmth engulfed his limbs and chest and made his head spin. The coating of dry prairie dust, and the soreness and stiffness of his legs and buttocks from weeks of riding, slowly soaked from his body. He stretched out and propped his head up at one end of the tub and the rest of his body was completely submerged. He closed his eyes and the warm water felt wonderfully soothing to his tired muscles. His eyes grew leaden. And yet he kept thinking of Travis, who was no more than four feet away on the other side of that partition. Travis moved around in his own tub; the water gently splashed as he did the same thing as Ethan, stretched out and relaxed with his head back. Even though the two of them were alone in that bathing room, separated by a thin piece of lacquered paper, neither of them spoke a word. Ethan heard Travis make a low groan, and he listened intently to the gentle sloshing sounds. He tried to make a mental image of Travis that fit the sounds and he had an erection – but he wasn't ashamed since nobody could see it under all the soapsuds. After about forty-five minutes soaking in sweet water, Travis began to wash himself. Ethan followed suit, sat up, and lathered the soap bar with his palms. He spread the lather all over his arms and chest, then stood up and tended to his lower extremities. Once he was clean, he got out of the bath dried himself with the thick hotel towels that were on a little stand by the tub and he put on his clean shirt. He had no choice but to put his dusty pants back on since he only had the one pair, but he shook them until they were free of the yellow dirt.

As they came out of the bathing room, Travis asked the man at the desk if he knew where they could find a seamstress in town. He gave them directions and they left the hotel and dropped off Ethan's pants to be mended. Next they stopped at the barbershop for a shave and a haircut.

Inside the barber was brushing the hair off Josh's shoulders with a whisk broom. He had just finished.

"Hi, guys!" Josh said. "Well, I got my shave, now I'm gonna go get my bath and you-know-what." Ethan knew what he was referring to, but Travis didn't or pretended he didn't.

"The guys are all going to get together at the saloon later to play some poker. You wanna join us, Ethan?" The cowboys already knew Travis didn't frequent saloons.

"No thanks. I think I'll just hang around with Travis."

"Okay then. Lovely evening to you!" He practically danced out of the shop and Travis took his place in the barber's chair.

They left the barbershop with faces as smooth as a newborn piglet, and smelling heavily of toilet water. Travis took Ethan to the nicest restaurant in town – Andre's Fine French Cuisine. It was a very neat and clean little restaurant with curtains in the windows, white tablecloths and a candle on each table. The floor was polished mahogany and the walls were dark and decorated with French paintings, a large one of Napoleon was the conspicuous centerpiece. The proprietor greeted them at the door and acted like he was Napoleon himself. A waitress seated them at a small table in the corner.

"Would the gentlemen like some wine with the dinner?" She spoke in a heavy French accent.

"Yes, please," Travis answered. The waitress retreated to the back room of the mostly empty restaurant.

"This place is as nice as some of the restaurants in San Antonio. I've only been in one like this a few times." Ethan pored over the menu. "Travis, the food here is kind of expensive. I don't know…"

"Don't worry about it, Ethan. The dinner is on me."

Ethan's eyes lingered for a moment on Travis's smile. Travis was being awfully generous.

The waitress returned with some hot bread and a bottle of red wine, which she poured into their glasses.

"Would you care to order now?"

Travis said, "I'll have the duck a la orange with vegetables."

"And you, sir?"

"I'll have the same, thank you."

The waitress glided back to the kitchen.

"How far have we come now, Travis? It's been a month since we started out. Are we a third of the way there?"

"Maybe a little more than a third of the way. We're well into the New Mexico Territory now. I'd say we've come about four hundred miles."

"Four hundred miles!" Ethan's eyes widened and he gripped the edges of the table. "I can't believe I'm that far away from home. I've never been that far away in my whole life."

Travis smiled at the display of awestruck innocence. "It should be about, oh, I would say another two and a half weeks and we'll cross into Colorado and then you'll start seeing some *really* beautiful country. The Rocky Mountains and lots of trees. Colorado is full of forests and mountains. I think you'll understand why I want to live there."

After dinner they went back to the hotel and up to their room. Ethan took the letters he was writing out of his saddlebags and sat down at the desk.

"I'm just going to finish writing these letters to my mother and Miss Peet before I turn in."

"Sure. You go right ahead. I'm just going to lie down and rest."

In his letters Ethan wrote about all he had seen and done thus far. He wrote about the trek across the desert, saving the cows, and all about the restaurant and hotel. He briefly mentioned his injury, making it sound more like a bruise. His mother was already worried enough. From outside came the sound of several men hollering, "Hee-yaah!" He pulled back the curtain and looked out the window, which was right beside the desk. Down below, across the street he saw Fred, Don and Joe stumbling out of the whorehouse. The three of them, holding one another up, staggered toward the saloon. Ethan let the curtain fall back into place. Travis breathed deeply and evenly. He gazed at that magnificent body in the flickering lamplight, all cleaned up and shaved. The gentle creases across his forehead, the sandy lashes against the smooth brown skin of his cheeks, which ended in the square cut of his jaw. He couldn't figure out why he felt such a connection with this man. It was closeness, but even stronger than family. Part of it might be that Ethan felt cared for by him. Travis was looking out for him, even taking care of him. This was a friendship like he had never experienced in his life. He closed his eyes and conjured up the image of Travis emerging out of the river, then he finished his letters, sealed them up and left them on the desk to be given to the town's postmaster in the morning. He quietly took off his boots, blew out the lamp and gently, so as not to wake Travis, lay down on the bed beside him. He then stared at the ceiling and waited for sleep to come.

Chapter Six

By the next afternoon they were back on the trail and were refreshed. Josh joined Ethan at the rear of the herd.

"Want a peppermint stick?" Josh asked, pointing a long white stick in Ethan's direction. "I bought a whole slew of them in town."

"Thanks." Ethan broke off a small piece, which he popped in his mouth. He stuffed the remainder into his shirt pocket.

"How was the whore?" Ethan asked just to make conversation.

"Whoa doggies!" Josh grinned with the peppermint stick between his teeth. "She was right somethin'! I got me a redhead this time." He went on to enthusiastically describe every detail of her anatomy, drawing it in the air with his candy, which instantly made Ethan regret that he had asked.

"You got family, Josh?"

"Sure. I got three older brothers in Abilene."

"Are they cowhands?"

"Nope. They're farmers and they all got wives."

"How about your folks?"

"They're in Abilene too."

"What do they think of your plans to become an actor?"

Josh stood up in the saddle, adjusted his privates, and sat back down. "Shit, I ain't never told 'em that! They think I'm stupid as it is. Folks just don't understand their kids."

Ethan bent over and stroked his horse's mane, then patted her neck. "Yeah, I know exactly what you mean."

"Why? Your pa don't understand you either?"

"He's dead, but he didn't much when he was alive. So what are you going to do, just strike off for New York without telling them?"

"I figure after I become famous and rich, I'll let 'em know and then they'll be proud."

Ethan nodded. It made sense. "How many plays have you seen?"

"About ten."

Ethan thought of Austen, Dickens, both Brontës, Poe, and asked, "What's your favorite?"

"The one I liked the best was called 'The Double-edged Sword.' It was about these two fellas who were best friends and they both were in love with the same girl. I think it was supposed to be in England or France or something 'cause there was a lot of swordfighting. They fought over this girl and she loved 'em both and couldn't choose which one to marry." Josh popped his peppermint stick back into his mouth, apparently finished with his story.

"Well?"

"Well, what?"

"How did the play end? Did she pick one of the guys or not?"

"Naw. They decided their friendship was more important than a woman, so neither one of them married her."

"And so she ended up alone?" It may have been a noble deed for the two men to step aside for one another, but the playwright was obviously a bachelor.

Josh said, "Aw, it's just a story," and broke into song.

From this valley they say you are going
We will miss your bright eyes and sweet smile

Ethan knew this song. His mother had sung it to him when he little. He began to sing along.

For they say you are taking the sunshine
That has brightened our path for a while

The two of them rode side by side, singing their hearts out behind twelve hundred cows.

Come and sit by my side if you love me
Do not hasten to bid me adieu
But remember the Red River Valley
And the cowboy who loved you so true

Virgil was riding just ahead of them on the right flank of the herd, and he stopped his horse. He pulled out his harmonica and played along. When they got to his position, he fell into rank and rode alongside for the next two verses of the song. From the left flank, Fred turned to look at the three of them. He sneered, and spit out a large stream of tobacco juice.

*   *   *

One morning in mid-July Ethan was finishing his breakfast when he saw Travis come out of his tent carrying clean clothes and a bar of soap. Ethan stuffed the rest of his breakfast into his mouth, deposited his tray and cup into the wash bin and headed through the wormwood bushes, past a small cluster of cottonwood trees and up an incline covered in tall grass. He tailed Travis to the river and crouched behind a big bushy elm.

Travis undressed and hung his clothes on a low limb. His back was to Ethan. He waded out into the middle of the river, the slow rippling current gently breaking against his thighs. He shivered a bit and let the clear water close over his body until he was fully immersed. He came up, lathered himself up, and washed his hair and chest. After he plunged into the water again, sending a film of soap downriver, he waded back toward the riverbank, further up the shore, where a limb blocked Ethan's view. Ethan ventured farther from the tree's protection. Travis's head came around and his eyes met Ethan's.

Ethan ducked back behind the tree and sank to his knees, face in his hands. He would have given every book in San Antonio to be able to disappear. He did the only thing he could think to do. He got up and ran like the wind back to camp.

Now, had Ethan not ducked back behind that tree, he would have seen that Travis was not mad at all. In fact he had even smiled.

Back at camp, Ethan packed up his things and folded up his

tent straightaway. He got on his horse and rode off to join the herd ahead of all the others. The rest of the cowboys wondered why he was in such a doggone hurry.

As the drive was getting underway, a hand clapped Ethan's shoulder. "Morning, Ethan."

Travis smiled and galloped off.

Ethan watched the dust rise behind the shrinking figure of Travis's horse. Was it possible that he hadn't seen him spying? Maybe he saw but didn't recognize him. Surely if Travis had seen him he would be furious – his friend, a peeping tom. Whatever the case, Ethan's mind was put to ease. Travis was still his friend and nothing changed between them.

"Uh-oh, look over there." Josh was pointing east. "A storm's comin'."

Way off on the horizon, dark clouds were advancing. There had been virtually no rain thus far on the cattle drive, just a few minor showers now and then. Rain would have been helpful in the desert, but now the herd came upon rivers and lakes most every day. A rainstorm would be nothing but a nuisance.

Chapter Seven

The storm overtook them the next day. Distant lightning and thunder made the herd skittish. As the lightning edged closer, Ethan began to get nervous, too. He had always enjoyed storms, but from the safety of shelter. As they traveled, giant jagged white seams split the sky directly ahead of them. They were so close that the thunder threw his heartbeat off. First there would be a flash on the right, then on the left, and eventually, the herd traveled in a corridor of lightning. Mr. Bennet obviously had not anticipated the quickness with which the storm would overtake them or surely he would have had them stop to set up a shelter. There was no way to stop or take cover. The herd was restless and unruly, and the horses kept getting spooked by the lightning. Small factions of the herd broke away and the cowboys would have to ride like hell bringing them back in.

And then the rain came. It came fast and violent and pounded for hours. The dry ground softened, absorbed the water, and turned to mud. Hooves and legs were slick and black, the entire outfit was soaked to the bone.

As it was, they finally had to stop for the night, several hours earlier than their usual stopping time and not at one of their scheduled camping sites. They had no choice. The herd was miserably bogged down and unbroken black clouds were in every direction. There was no dry wood to start a fire, so the cowboys pitched their tents in the mud and were served cold beans, bread and jerky, which they ate inside their tents before going to sleep.

Ethan was lucky he didn't have guard duty that night, for more good reasons than just the rain. The landscape was not such that the herd could be blocked and settled in; they camped on wide-open prairie, and the man on guard had to circle the restless herd and pull back the cows that tried to wander off. The unlucky cowpoke who got the first shift was Josh. Soaked to the skin, water pouring off the rim of his hat, he pulled his jacket tight around himself and rode off into the night.

Ethan tried to sleep, but found he was cold and his soaked clothes soon transferred the water to his bedroll.

After the third straight day of rain, Ethan was more miserable than he had ever been in his life. Both sets of Ethan's clothes were completely soaked. During the day the temperature dropped so much that he wore both shirts to keep warm, and the nights were downright frigid. The rain let up some when they stopped to set up camp the third night, but with everything so waterlogged it was still impossible to get a fire going. The cowboys were in bad spirits and snapped at each other. A few brief fistfights broke out, usually between Fred and anybody who crossed his line of sight.

Inside his tent, Ethan shivered in his bedroll, teeth chattering. He had been cold the past two nights, but this was different. This coldness went straight down to his bones.

Out of desperation he got up and went to Travis's tent.

"Travis," he called at the tent flap. "It's me."

Travis poked his head out of the tent. "What's the matter, Ethan?"

"I'm really, really cold," he said, still shivering.

"Come on in here." Travis opened up his tent and Ethan ducked in. The pup tent was only really big enough for one.

"First of all we need to get you out of these wet shirts, and everything else."

Ethan struggled to take off his boots. Travis helped him out by unbuttoning his jacket and two shirts. Finally, in the darkness, Ethan had been stripped naked. Travis then took off all his own clothes and left all the clothing in a pile at the foot of the tent. He and Ethan slid into the bedroll together. They lay face to face and Travis embraced Ethan to warm him up. He rubbed his hands up and down Ethan's back and shoulders. The warmth of Travis body began to radiate into Ethan's body and he stopped shivering.

Once he was warm again, the reality of the situation set in, and he could feel the nakedness of Travis's body pressed up against him. He got a strange, euphoric, tingly sensation all over his body. It was the most fantastic feeling he had ever had. They lay entwined in each other's arms, not speaking. Travis caressed Ethan's back, then his face, his ear, and chest. Ethan instinctively felt he had permission to do the same to Travis. Occasionally one of them would doze off for a few seconds, but it wasn't until morning that Ethan actually fell asleep.

He awoke when Travis disengaged himself from their embrace and slipped out of the bedroll. He pulled on his clothes, which wasn't easy in such a small place.

"You stay right here and get some more sleep," he whispered to Ethan. Ethan had no choice; Travis took all Ethan's clothes with him and left the tent.

He awoke again when Travis opened the tent flap and tossed in his clothes. They were dry and warm. He could hear the crackle and hiss of the first fire in three days. Breakfast was frying. He got dressed and followed the smell of bacon and coffee out of the tent. The rain was gone and the clouds were breaking up. There might even be some sunshine. A hundred questions needled in Ethan's mind, questions he wanted to ask Travis, but everyone was milling around, eating breakfast and packing up the camp.

They got back on the trail and began to move on. The rain had turned the trail into one long bog. On each of the three days of the storm, they had traveled less than half the distance they would have made in good weather, so Mr. Bennet drove them hard. Bunny tried to steer the wagon clear of any serious mud pits, but he got stuck twice and the cowboys all had to work together to push him out. Finally, late that afternoon, the sun came out.

"Finally!" Ethan said to Josh. "I thought that storm would

never end."

Josh nodded and coughed. It was a bad sounding cough, phlegmy and far down in his chest.

"You okay, Josh?"

"I'm fine. Just caught a cold from all the rain."

"But you're feeling okay, otherwise?"

"Yeah, I'm fine. But what about you? You've been yawning all morning. Didn't you rest well last night?"

"No. I had trouble getting to sleep."

Chapter Eight

Now, in northern New Mexico Territory, the landscape was beginning to change. The slow, lazy Pecos cut a winding path alongside the trail. The plains gave way to mountains and small patches of forest broke the horizon. The sun set and the stars emerged in the deep indigo sky. Near the riverbank, in a clearing partially encompassed by foliage, a roaring campfire flung sparks into the night. Sixteen men were gathered round, seated on crates and rocks, finishing the last of their supper. Josh coughed again.

"You still have that cold, huh?" Ethan asked, setting his plate aside.

Josh recovered himself and spit into the fire. "Yep. I just can't seem to shake it." He looked over at the old cook chewing on a grisly hunk of beef. "How come they call you Bunny? Is that a nickname or something?"

Patrick, David, and several others starting laughing.

"Just never you mind!" Bunny retorted.

"Ain't you boys ever heard the story of how Bunny got his name?" Mr. Bennet said. "You don't mind if I tell them the story, do you Bunny?"

"Go ahead. You're gonna tell it anyway, whether I want you to or not." Bunny turned his back on them so he could eat the rest of his dinner in peace.

"Well," Mr. Bennet said, "it was about, oh I'd say five or six years ago, we were out on this very same cattle drive and several of the fellas were out huntin' and they shot this here rabbit. Well as it turns out the rabbit was on her way back to her nest when they shot her and so they found her nest full of little bunnies. So they brought back the dead rabbit and all the little bunnies for Bunny to cook 'em in a stew. Well, you see, Bunny just couldn't bring himself to killin' those poor little bunnies, so he put 'em in a box and raised 'em up. And he guarded them, for fear somebody would skin 'em and eat 'em. And so since he spent the whole darn cattle drive protectin' those little bunnies, everyone just started calling *him* Bunny and the name stuck."

The cowboys who hadn't heard the story before now joined in the laughter with the others and Bunny got up and grabbed the bowls and stalked off to the wagon.

*   *   *

Late that night Ethan woke to Travis's voice at his tent flap. He pulled it open.

"Can I sleep in your tent tonight?" Travis whispered.

He let Travis in and in the darkness they undressed and entwined themselves in Ethan's bedroll. They caressed each other and gently explored each other's bodies with their hands. Ethan was filled with euphoria. They settled down into a tender embrace, and with his mouth right up against Ethan's ear Travis whispered four words. The *only* words that were spoken that night – "I love you, Ethan."

Love. Is that what this was all about? Ethan wondered what Travis meant by those words. After all there were many different types of love. There was the familial type that he was most familiar with. Mothers loving their children. Children loving their parents and grandparents and aunts and brothers and sisters. But Ethan had never been told he had been loved by a man before. Not by his brother, not even by his father. But he had read about good friends loving one another in books. Sydney certainly loved Charles in *A Tale of Two Cities*. Could this be the type of love Travis meant? Then of course there was the romantic type of love between Romeo and Juliet, or Elizabeth and Mr. Darcy. There was no such thing as romantic love between two men. What if instead, Romeo loved Mercutio, and

110

Mr. Darcy loved Mr. Bingley? Ethan lay awake long into the night. He knew Travis had fallen asleep by his gentle, even breaths. He would definitely have to ask Travis about it tomorrow.

*   *   *

The next day's brilliant sun struck the landscape. Cloudless sky and cooler air abounded. The mountains loomed up in the west and lush green forests surrounded the trail. Ethan felt wonderful just to be alive; and Travis was right, this was the most beautiful country in the whole world. The well-fed and watered herd chipped along at a pace of at least twenty miles a day. As the sun began to sink, Mr. Bennet picked out a nice clearing. The herd was penned in between an embankment and a pine forest. They set up camp in a small clearing in the trees, comfortably blanketed with needles.

After they had pitched their tents and were waiting for supper, Ethan told Travis he would like to ask him some questions. Travis nodded as though he had been expecting this. "Come on, follow me," he said and picked his way deep into the woods. When he was sure they were out of earshot of the camp and could speak in privacy, he stopped. Ethan leaned up against a tree.

"Travis, I don't understand what's happening between us."

"Shh." Travis came up to him and took Ethan's hands into his own. "Close your eyes, Ethan."

"Why?"

"Trust me. Just close your eyes. Please."

Ethan closed them. Travis's lips pressed up against his own. Ethan flinched.

"What are you doing?"

"Ethan, it's okay. Just relax. Now close your eyes. Trust me. It will be okay."

Ethan closed his eyes. He felt Travis gently kiss him on the lips. He relaxed his own lips and began to go with the feeling. It was a phenomenal sensation – softness, warmth and wetness all together; and both sharing the same breath.

"Now," Travis said, "I will answer your questions."

Ethan said, "I'm confused about what's happening with us. I

111

don't know what it all means."

Travis looked up at the sky for a moment, then back at Ethan. "I'll try to explain this as simply as I can. Ethan, you and I are two very special kind of men. We're not like other men. Whereas most men are drawn to and mate with women, we are drawn to and mate with other men."

Ethan had never heard of such a thing. "So when you said you loved me, you were talking about romantic love?"

"Exactly. The same kind of love that normally exists between a man and a woman, can sometimes happen between two men. You know when I told you that there are things about me that my parents don't know and couldn't understand?"

"Yes."

"This is what I was talking about."

"But you said you had been with women."

"I have. But I've also been with men in the same way and I know that being with a man is what is right for me. But until I met you, I never was in love."

"Is there a name for what we are? I mean what do you call this thing?"

"Well, the Bible refers to us as sodomites. Have you read the Bible?"

"No. My parents never went to church."

"Well, actually that's probably very good. You haven't been engrained with teachings that would make you feel guilty about something you have no control over. Anyway what I need to tell you next is very important.

"People don't understand us; and what they don't understand they hate; and what they hate they make laws against. Sodomy is against the law and the punishment for people who are caught is severe. Some states even put sodomites to death. That's why you have to keep this secret. If people find out, they will do harm to you. You can't trust anyone with our secret. Not even your mother. The only people you can ever tell this to are others like us, but even then you have to be careful because some of them are filled with so much guilt for what they are that they will betray you to ease their own conscience. You have to be very careful choosing who you can trust."

The breeze rustled the pine needles and an owl hooted from a nearby tree. Ethan was solemn. "How can you tell who will betray you?"

"It's something you have to develop an instinct for. You can learn to read people. I can't really explain it, but you just know who's okay and who's not."

Ethan just stood there for a little while, watching the owl as it took flight and disappeared into the woods. Finally he said, "How do people like us live?"

"Live?"

"I mean, how do they get by when everybody hates them?"

Travis hesitated. He leaned his head back against the tree trunk and searched for his words. "One way is two men who are in love will go off and live in a home together in a secluded area where they don't have to deal with the fear of being discovered. Inside their home they are mates, but outside they just act as friends and nobody suspects any different. Or they'll just marry a woman and then go off and mate with other men in secret. They sometimes even find men who will take money to mate with them."

"Like whores?"

"Yes, like male whores. Since they are paid for their services they keep the secret. And then there are men who will marry women and never give in to their natural desires to be with other men. These men are the most dangerous, because they are so filled with hate for the desires that are inside of them, they will turn that hate on you. And then there is one other method that I've only seen a couple times. Two males who are in love with each other will get together with two females who are in love with each other and – "

"Females in love with each other?"

"Of course. If it could happen to two men, why couldn't women do the same? Anyway, each of the men will marry one of the women and the four of them will live in a homestead together. To the outside world, they are just two normal married couples, but inside the house they are actually paired off differently."

"But why? What's the point of what they are doing?"

"For protection. Nobody would ever suspect the truth."

Travis moved closer and took Ethan's hands into his own. "What I want most for you, Ethan, is for you to be happy. So no matter what anybody ever tells you, there's nothing wrong with you. You have nothing to feel guilty for. Despite the laws, the Bible, and the whole world thinking sodomy is immoral and degenerate, I assure you, they are wrong. We are not evil, bad people. We are decent good people just like everyone else. We're just misunderstood. Someday maybe things will change and people will be made to understand this, but until then the only way we can survive in this hateful world is in complete secrecy."

Still holding Ethan's hands, Travis looked away. Ethan could see the pain behind his eyes, and hear it in his voice. He loosened his grip, put his arms around Travis and pulled him close. They stood, cheek to cheek in a tight embrace until Travis finally said, "We had better be getting back to camp. Supper's probably ready."

Before they went back Ethan couldn't resist the urge to have just one more kiss. So he closed his eyes, gave Travis a quick kiss on the lips and then dashed off back to the camp with Travis right behind him.

Chapter Nine

"Ethan, are you in there?" The voice outside Ethan's tent was hushed so as not to wake the other men.

Ethan and Travis both sat up, alarmed out of their slumber. Travis's warning had made him skittish. Ethan stuck his head out of the tent flap keeping it clinched tight around his neck.

"What's the matter, Josh?"

"I need you to help me out, Ethan. I got a plan to fix David real good. Come on out a give me a hand, will ya?"

"Okay. Just give me a few minutes. I got to put my boots on." Ethan ducked his head back into the tent, fumbled around in the dark for his clothes, and got dressed as quickly as he could. Travis stayed put in the bedroll.

Outside the tent, Josh was waiting with an armload of clothing.

"What are you going to do with those?" he asked.

"You'll see." He led Ethan to a nearby pine tree and dropped the clothing in a pile at the base. "Give me a leg up."

Ethan looked up at the tree. The nearest branches were about nine or ten feet off the ground. Ethan interlocked his fingers to make a stirrup, and Josh stepped into his hands with one foot and put his knee onto Ethan's shoulder. He balanced himself against the tree trunk, then put his foot on Ethan's other shoulder and stood up.

"OUCH!"

"Shhh. You'll wake everyone up!"

"Well, your boots are digging into my shoulders."

Josh grabbed hold of the nearest branch, and with agility, swung himself onto it.

"Throw me up a shirt."

Ethan picked one of David's shirts from the pile, wadded it up into a ball and tossed it up. The shirt came up two feet away from Josh. Josh tried to catch it, slipped and almost fell out of the tree.

"Sorry." Ethan threw it again, this time into Josh's hands. Josh tied the sleeves together into a loose knot around a tree branch. He then moved over a few feet and asked for David's pants. He draped a leg on either side of a large limb so the pants straddled it. He climbed farther up the tree and called for David's vest.

"Where'd you get all these clothes, Josh?"

"I took 'em from David's tent. Everybody knows he don't like to sleep with his clothes on. The rest of 'em I got out of his saddlebags. I took every single thing he's got. Now throw me up them chaps."

Josh proceeded to hang both shirts, two pair of pants, chaps, gunbelt and holster into the tree. He wedged David's boots into a crook where the trunk divided. He kept climbing higher until he ran out of items. Then at the highest point, he took the hat off his head and hung it up. Until that moment, Ethan hadn't even realized that Josh had been wearing David's hat the whole time. Josh climbed back down the tree and stepped back to admire his work. The tree was fully decorated. It looked like a cowboy had exploded all over the tree.

"Dang! I can't wait 'til tomorrow morning. The guys are all gonna get a kick out of this." Josh was restraining himself from laughing out loud in anticipation of the payoff of his prank. Ethan agreed with Josh that it was going to be a good one. David would be mad all right, but he wouldn't hurt anybody over it, like Fred or Patrick.

"Thanks, Ethan, I better get back to the herd now. I won't tell no one you helped me." He strolled away, chuckling to himself.

Ethan went back into his tent and undressed again.

"Did you hear what we were doing out there?"

"I heard. Good Lord, what will that kid think of next?" Travis held the bedroll open and pulled Ethan into the warmth.

The next morning most of the men were sitting around the breakfast fire drinking their coffee and waiting for David to wake up and come out of his tent. Most of them congratulated Josh on work well done. Mr. Bennet had seen the decorated tree and laughed; he didn't mind pranks and horseplay just so long as it didn't interfere with any actual work. A yell woke the peaceful morning.

"SOMEBODY STOLE MY CLOTHES!" He bolted out of his tent wearing nothing but orange longjohns that sagged to his knees. "SOMEBODY DONE STOLE ALL MY CLOTHES!"

"Ain't nobody stole your clothes," Patrick said. "They just went out to get some fresh air."

All the men burst into raucous laughter. David looked up, saw his clothes strewn about the tree and turned beet red. He was mad as a Texas bull.

"Goddamn you, Josh!"

"Me?" Josh said. "What makes you think I done it?"

"I know you's the one who done it! I know you had guard duty last night. Now how the hell am I supposed to get the stuff down?"

"I don't know David," Mr. Bennet said. "But you had better hurry up and figure it out, because were movin' out in twenty minutes. And I know you don't want to be seen ridin' into town in nothin' but your undergarments!" There was another round of laughter, and David paced back and forth under the tree trying to figure out what to do, muttering curses at Josh. None of the men offered to help, and went about their breakfast.

*   *   *

At the start of August, the trail ascended into Colorado, bringing the freshest pine-scented air and the clearest sapphire skies yet. The Rocky Mountains soared to the west of them with tips like granite and bases like green velvet. Green grass carpeted the land as far as the eye could see, interrupted only by pine trees. Deep indigo lakes and clear streams irrigated the valley. Ethan agreed with Travis – this was paradise.

But what made this the happiest time in Ethan's life was love. Ten times each day Travis would drop to the back of the herd and point out some beautiful landmark or some pretty vista – the way sunlight clung to an escarpment. They had a routine of tent-visiting: only on nights when they didn't have guard duty, one or the other would wait until all the other men were fast asleep, and then would quietly slip inside the other's tent. The next morning they would exit the tent discreetly at separate times. To all the other men, they just appeared to be good buddies.

The one dark cloud during this time was Josh. Travis took to helping him pitch his tent every night, and started to share his worry with Ethan. Sometimes he went into such a coughing fit that he had to get off his horse so he could hack up all the phlegm. He looked peaked and tired, and twenty years older. He was so exhausted every night that he would retreat to his tent right after supper and force himself to get up the next morning.

A few days later he got off his horse to cough up phlegm, and gagged on it.

"Josh, you're really sick," Ethan said. "I'm going to go and get Mr. Bennet."

Josh raised his hand, struggling to speak while he gagged. "No! I'll be fine in a minute."

"Don't you think you should see a doctor?"

"No."

"You're not getting any better. You should quit the drive and go see a doctor. I'm sure he could give you medicine to cure whatever's wrong with you."

He spit out some phlegm and wiped his mouth. "I can't."

"Why not?"

"Because then I won't get paid. I want to finish the drive so I can get my money."

"I'm sure Mr. Bennet would pay you for the work you've done so far."

Josh briskly hopped back up on his horse but fumbled on the saddle. "Of course he won't. Didn't you read your contract? You only get paid if you finish the drive. No exceptions."

"Even if you're this ill? That's ridiculous!"

"That's the way it is. Don't go tell Mr. Bennet. I'll make it just fine."

*　　*　　*

Late that night Travis woke Ethan up for guard duty. Ethan crawled out of his tent and strolled over to the embankment they were using as a guard post. Travis followed him. The cows were sleeping so they just sat down in the grass – Travis with his knees drawn up and his arms resting on them, Ethan cross-legged and still rubbing the sleep out of his eyes. There was quiet lowing, and the occasional rustling and thud of a hoof, but the herd was mostly asleep.

"How did you know about me, Travis?"

Travis plucked a foxtail from the ground and slipped the stem in his mouth. Then he stretched out his legs and leaned back on one elbow so that he was facing Ethan.

"You mean how did I know you were like me?"

"Yeah. When did you figure it out?"

"The first time I saw you, when I came into the store."

The remaining sleepiness evaporated. "What? That's impossible! How could you tell?"

"Just by the way you looked at me when I came in. I could see it in your eyes. I don't know, it was sort of a longing look. Like you were sizing up my features. I've seen that look enough to know how to recognize it. So I thought to myself, 'Here's a handsome young man who's looking for my kind of romance.'" Travis pulled the foxtail from his teeth and dropped his gaze. "I feel kind of embarrassed telling you this but that's when I made a plan to win you over."

"This was all part of a plan?" It was like in a Jane Austen novel where the lady manipulates the man into falling in love with her, or like Miss Peet's machinations. Yet Ethan wasn't upset.

"Yep. I made a plan to woo you. I had to be cautious and take it very slow because I didn't want to scare you away before you were ready. Remember that day I came to the store to talk to you while you were all alone in there? I lounged around town all morning waiting for the store owner – what was his name? Mr. Simpson? – to leave on his errands so I could catch you alone."

Travis returned the foxtail to his lips. The craggy outline of his shoulder and hip resembled a moonlit mountain range.

Ethan said, "I had no idea."

"And then of course asking you to come on the cattle drive. And then when I was bathing in the river…"

Ethan's face heated up. "I thought you saw me, but you didn't say anything about it."

"That's when I knew you were ready for the next step. It made me so happy that you wanted me as much as I wanted you." His voice had a hint of flirtation. "I think the plan worked out perfectly. Don't you?"

"It sure did. I'm glad you did it. I love you, Travis."

"I love you too, Ethan."

Ethan plucked the foxtail out of Travis's teeth and kissed him. After a few minutes of silence, Ethan spoke again.

"Tell me about your first time with another man."

"Come on Ethan, you don't really want to know all about that. It's history. It doesn't mean anything to me now."

"Yeah, but you know all about my first time, because it was with you. I want to know about yours."

"Okay, okay. I don't think you're going to like this story, but here goes. It was probably about three years ago. It was some time after I had broken up with the girl I told you about. I was going from town to town finding work as a ranch hand, and going on cattle drives. I had been with quite a few different women by then. I knew I had desires for other men, but I kept them buried inside. I was ashamed of my feelings. I was very different from the way I am now. My parents were churchgoing, God-fearing people and I had been taught that sodomy was the greatest of all sins, and sodomites were possessed by the devil himself. So it only made me hate what was inside of me.

"Well, anyway, working around so many other ranch hands and cowpokes, naturally I came across quite a few very handsome men and of course I would notice them and I suppose I even developed a few crushes, but I always felt guilty about my fantasies and often I would seek out the companionship of a woman to try and prove to myself that I wasn't really that way. And women were easy. It wasn't hard to find a woman to bed me, they were only too eager. Looking back, I feel very bad that I used so many women in that way.

"But I guess you're waiting to hear about my first time with a *man*, aren't you?"

Ethan nodded.

"It was in a little town in Texas. Hell, I can't even remember the name, but it was just outside Houston. I was in a saloon – "

"I thought you didn't frequent saloons."

"I don't now. But as I said, I was a different person then. There was a timid little man who played the piano. He was older than me. He may have been thirty-five or so. To be truthful, I didn't find him at all to be good-looking. He was sweaty and he wore glasses."

"He would be your first? But why, if you didn't like him?"

"I'm getting to that. Well, I sat at the bar, drinking. I was really feeling the effects of the whiskey. I looked around the room, eyeing some of the other men. Meanwhile, he was eyeing me. When I saw him, I immediately recognized it in his look. He looked away. But I knew I had found another sinner. He continued to watch while he played the piano, looking away every time I looked back at him. He wanted me and I knew it. I was drunk and my desire to be with a man, *any man,* at this time was very great. So I stayed at the saloon until they closed it up and I waited outside for him. I asked him if he wanted to go somewhere. He was very nervous, but he agreed. So we broke into the livery stable and did it in the hayloft. There was no love, just mating, and then we went our separate ways and I never saw him again."

Ethan was speechless. It was far from his own experience and he felt bad for Travis and hung his head, staring at the ground. Travis, noticing Ethan was disturbed, gently hoisted Ethan's chin with his thumb and forefinger and looked him in the eyes.

"I told you that you wouldn't like it. But as unromantic as the whole experience was, it did have one benefit. It proved to me that I was meant to be with a man. It was a turning point in my life. I never mated with another woman after that, and in my mind, I began to question the beliefs I was brought up with."

"What about your other experiences with men? Were they just like the first one?"

Travis held up his index finger. "Shhh…"

Ethan frowned. Travis cocked his head toward the camp. Someone was walking towards them and was nearly within earshot – Don. He stopped, turned towards a bush, unfastened his trousers and emptied his bladder. Still half asleep, he turned back and shuffled to his tent.

Travis resumed the conversation, in a lower voice "No, the other men were not like the first. After that I began to seek out men who I could really care about. And I met people who taught me some things about how people like us can survive in this world. The same things I've told you."

Ethan gazed out into the herd and then up at the night sky, contemplating everything Travis had just told him. Before he could comprehend it all, Travis stood.

"I guess I'd better hit the sack. I've got to get some sleep. 'Night, Ethan."

"Good night, Travis."

Chapter Ten

The next day broke over the treetops. The sky was the perfect shade of azure, scattered with billowy white clouds. The air smelled of pine needles and the sun warmed Ethan's face. He thought about all he had been through on this trip. If someone would have told him four months ago that he would be driving cows through this beautiful land and would have fallen deeply in love with a cowboy, he would have laughed. It's funny how life could change so completely, so quickly. For the first time, a new thought entered his head: What was going to happen after the cattle drive? Would he go back to working in Mr. Simpson's store and spending his evenings cooped up in his little room reading his books? Would he and Travis part ways and would Travis go on to other cattle drives without him? He couldn't bear the thought of separation from Travis. His old life no longer fit. He couldn't spend too much time thinking about it because there was a lot of hard work to do.

The herd was traveling northward at a substantial incline, so they all worked hard to keep the cows in line. They had a tendency to scatter when they were made to climb. That afternoon, a bunch of cows on Josh's side of the rear flank strayed off and Josh wasn't doing anything to bring them back in.

"Josh! Your cows are getting away!"

Josh didn't respond, so Ethan rode over to Josh's position to see what was wrong. As he came up to him he saw that Josh was pale as a ghost and his head bobbed back and forth. His eyes fluttered like he was straining to stay conscious.

"Josh?"

Josh collapsed. He rolled right off his horse and hit the ground, unconscious. Ethan yelled for help. All the cowboys left their positions and gathered round. Josh lay on his back with his arms and legs sprawled out in all directions. The cowboys huddled around him as though he was going to die right there. Mr. Bennet broke through the group with Travis, dismounted and knelt.

"What happened here?"

"He passed out," Ethan replied.

"What are we gonna do now?" Patrick asked.

"He's really sick. Somehow we gotta get him to a doctor," Virgil said.

Mr. Bennet folded his arms, sighed and shook his head. "Well, I'm open for suggestions, boys. What do you think we should do? Should we turn back or go forward?"

"We might find a doctor in one of them little villages we passed," Patrick said.

"And we might not," Mr. Bennet countered. "Pueblo is still some fifty miles ahead. It'll take us at least three days to get there at top speed."

"He won't make it three days." They all looked up to see who had just spoken. It was Travis, who had been quietly observing. "You've noticed how he's breathing. His lungs are full of fluid. He's got pneumonia."

"I don't see what difference it makes," Fred spoke up. "Look at him. He's a goner. Let's just put him in the wagon, and when he croaks we'll bury him."

"YOU BITE YOUR TONGUE!" Mr. Bennet bellowed. "We're not gonna let this man die! Do any of you here have any doctorin' skills at all?"

They all shook their heads. While everyone was pondering what to do, Ethan knelt down beside Josh. He was out cold but he continued to struggle for his breath, fighting a raspy gurgling in his lungs. Beads of sweat had formed on his brow. Ethan straightened out Josh's arms and legs and cupped his hand underneath Josh's head to make him more comfortable.

Mr. Bennet held up his hand to silence the men's arguments.

"Boys, here's the situation, We can't go back because it's too big a gamble that we'll even find a doctor, and Pueblo's too far ahead to get him there in time. The way I see it, there's only one thing to do. Somebody's gonna have to take him on ahead to Pueblo."

"I'll go," said Travis. "After all, I know this territory pretty well and Cleo's the fastest horse we've got. I can get him to Pueblo by sundown."

"Very well then. It's settled," Mr. Bennet said. "How do you want to take him? Should we sling him over his horse and have you lead him?"

"No. That's too slow and he'd fall off for sure. He'll have to ride with me on Cleo."

Travis mounted his horse and asked them to bring Josh up. They hoisted Josh's limp body into the saddle directly behind him, and he positioned Josh's arms around his waist and tied his hands together with a length of rope, so he wouldn't fall off, even if he remained unconscious.

They took Travis's canteen and filled it with water, and gave him two extra. Bunny stuffed jerky and several cans of beans into his saddle bags.

"Okay, Travis," Mr. Bennet said. "Ride like the wind. We'll see you in Pueblo!"

And with that Travis took off like a jockey on a racehorse. In a few minutes he had disappeared over the hills.

*   *   *

Other than Travis, Josh was Ethan's only friend. The other men were rough and crude – but Virgil was the least threatening of the bunch, so Ethan was glad when he took over Josh's position at the rear.

"Do you think Josh is going to be all right?" he asked.

"I don't know. He was lookin' pretty bad."

"But if Travis gets him to a doctor in time, they'll be able to fix him up, won't they?"

"Yeah. I guess so."

"I think he's going to be fine." Virgil's pessimism made Ethan even more sullen. "You just wait. I'll bet when we get to Pueblo, he'll be sitting up in bed eating soup. He might even be ready to rejoin the cattle drive."

Virgil shrugged. "I hope so."

"When are you getting married, Virgil?"

Virgil perked up immediately. "Just as soon as we get to Cheyenne. My Betsy will be waiting for me there."

"You're really in love with her, aren't you?"

"Well, yeah. Men are supposed to love the girls they're gonna marry. And I'm getting' me a mighty fine woman, too. A man needs a woman to cook and clean for him, and to raise up his youngins. After all, that's what they're here for."

"Uh-huh."

"You're just a tadpole now, but you'll see. One day you'll get you a pretty young girl who'll do the same for you. And you'll love her just like I love my Betsy. You'll see."

Ethan nodded and tugged at the brim of his hat. It just didn't feel right without Travis around. The day had started out so joyous and beautiful, but now it had changed so completely, so quickly. The landscape was the same, but somehow the pine trees and clouds were lonely and desolate. Pueblo couldn't come soon enough. That night he ate supper all by himself. His spirits were down and the men all gathered around the campfire making their usual conversation, and nothing anybody said about guns and poker and women held his interest. Feeling drowsy, Ethan went to bed early.

The next day, the Rockies looked distant and foreboding, lonely peaks still capped with last winter's dirty snow. The surrounding pine trees were gnarled and menacing; their pinecones and dead needles skittering and crunching wetly beneath the horses' hooves. Even the wide open sky seemed empty, an open mouth that swallowed every last bird.

Sometime in the early afternoon, a shout carried back from the front of the herd. Somebody had seen Travis up ahead.

Ethan turned to Virgil. "You think it's possible we're already coming up to Pueblo?"

Virgil looked confused, then shook his head.

It had only been a day and a half. Maybe Travis had already been to Pueblo, left Josh with a doctor, and had ridden back to join them.

Ethan abandoned the herd and galloped ahead with the rest of the men to find Travis. Way off in the distance, Travis sat on the ground by a large oak. He spurred his horse to go faster. Something didn't seem right. Cleo grazed nearby. As he got nearer, he slowed down and the other men drew up next to him. Travis stood to greet them. At his feet was a dug-up patch of ground.

"I'm sorry guys," Travis said. "I didn't make it in time."

Ethan noticed that the other cowboys had removed their hats, so he removed his, too. For a long while nobody spoke. Finally Mr. Bennet broke the silence.

"We should all say a few words for Josh and then we'll carve out a marker for his grave. And then we'll need to round up the herd and move on."

Travis gave Mr. Bennet a sharp look, but he didn't say anything. One by one the cowboys eulogized Josh. Most of them said things about how good natured he was and how he always made them laugh with his clowning. It was all just meaningless words spoken to the air.

When Ethan's turn came, he was at a loss for words. He spoke slowly at first, and then with greater ease. "Josh was my friend. When I first joined the cattle drive, I barely knew anyone, but Josh was the first one to talk to me and make me feel welcome. I never heard him say a mean word to anybody. He wanted to go to New York to act on the stage, and I know he would have been a great actor. Entertaining people and making them laugh brought him so much happiness. I've never known anyone to die as young as he, or as unfairly, but I only hope that wherever he is, he knows that he lives on in the memory of our friendship."

After all the men had said all they could, Virgil carved out the marker. He took a broken piece of floorboard from the supply wagon and with his knife made neat, bold letters deep into the wood.

HERE LIES
JOSH KELLY
19 YEARS OLD
DIED AUGUST 10, 1878
REST IN PEACE

Since nobody knew when Josh's birthday was they couldn't figure out what year he had been born, so they just went on what they had. They pounded the board into the ground and mounded stones around its base. They all said their goodbyes to Josh, climbed back up on their horses and went to collect the scattered herd.

Chapter Eleven

Cowboys had to bear at least one cross: loss of life on the trail. The veterans had almost come to expect it, as though the trail gods demanded a human sacrifice for passage. But no matter how many times it happened, it never got any easier, and the remaining journey into Pueblo was a solemn one.

The only one who didn't appear to be affected was Fred, who continued his insolence and bullying. Travis rode off by himself and talked to no one, not even Ethan.

That night they set up camp in a small valley between the mountains, and Travis still kept to himself and pitched his own tent at the edge of camp. As soon as he finished his work, he went directly to bed without waiting for supper. There would be no tent visiting tonight. Even though Ethan longed to be held in Travis's arms right now, he knew that Travis needed his solitude to grieve. When Bunny called everyone to supper, Ethan joined the rest of the cowboys. "It just don't seem right, not seeing Josh at the head of the chow line," David said. The meal was mirthless as they were eating more out of necessity than enjoyment, and no one except Fred had a large appetite that night. After finishing the meal, they sat around the campfire and stared into the flames. "I keep thinkin' on that story he told us about riding forty miles to look at a girl sittin' on a porch," Virgil said with a woeful smile. After nearly two months on the trail they had all gotten to know Josh well, and some expressed sorrow for his family and Mr. Bennet stated that he would see that all Josh's personal belongings were taken to his parents in Abilene.

Ethan listened in silence to the conversation, too affected to participate. When he turned in for the night, he needed Travis but he knew that he couldn't have him, not tonight. He lay in his bedroll thinking about Josh tracing a woman's figure in the air with his peppermint stick, or climbing around in that tree with David's clothes. He felt a wave of gut wrenching sorrow begging to be released, but no tears came. He finally purged thoughts from his head one by one, until he fell asleep.

Late the next day, they arrived in Pueblo. This time there was no hooting and hollering as the cowboys closed in on the town. They silently entered. The reddish adobe buildings lined the dusty streets, with pine trees scattered about. Most still visited the saloon and the brothel, but they didn't do it with the enthusiasm of the last town.

Ethan and Travis went directly to the hotel and checked in. Travis sat down on the bed. Ethan sat in the chair across from him. They still had not spoken since the incident, and Ethan didn't know whether to say anything or not – but Travis looked like he wanted to unburden himself, so Ethan just waited. Travis stared at the floor.

"Ethan, it was just horrible," he finally said.

"What happened out there?"

"I rode Cleo as fast a pace as I could without wearing her out. Every two or three hours I stopped to give her a breather and check on Josh. He was so sick he barely knew who I was. His lungs were so full of crap he had a hard time breathing. I tried to get him to take some water but he'd choke. So off we'd go again for another run. Then finally the last time I stopped, Josh was limp behind me. He wasn't breathing, so I got him down off the horse and laid him on the ground." With his elbows on his knees Travis hung his head and rested his forehead in his palms. "I wanted so bad to be able to save him. But I failed." He looked back up at Ethan, his face contorted with pain. "I just sat there beside him for a long time. After a while I knew that I had to bury him. I didn't even have a damn shovel! I had to find some rocks to dig with. It took me the better part of a day just to dig a hole big enough and deep enough to give him a proper burial." He sighed and looked away, staring into empty space, and shifted to a quieter tone. "That night I slept by his grave, then I rationed my food and water and waited for you guys to show up.

"Why couldn't I have saved him? For God's sake, he was only nineteen years old! We all saw that he was ailing. Why didn't we get him to a doctor earlier?"

"He wouldn't have gone," Ethan said. "I told him he should quit the cattle drive and go to a doctor and get some medicine but he said he didn't want to lose his pay."

"I could have *forced* him to go. He'd still be alive if I had." Travis's eyes were wet.

"It's not your fault, Travis. Anyway, isn't it Mr. Bennet's responsibility to look after the cowboys and get them doctoring when they need it?"

"Bennet doesn't give a fuck about anything but making sure that damned herd makes it to market!"

Tears streamed down Travis's cheeks. Ethan could think of nothing to say to comfort him, so moved over to the bed and put his arm around his shoulders. Travis buried his face into Ethan's chest and cried. All the emotions he had been holding back for the last few days had finally come to the surface. Ethan just held him and gently stroked his hair.

Once he'd regained his composure, Travis said, "I really wanted to be able to save him."

"I know. We all wanted that."

As they continued to embrace, the nurturing turned into passion and the tears tuned into kisses. Travis only let go of Ethan long enough to quickly lock the door. They tore off each other's clothes. They smothered each other with kisses, from their foreheads all the way down to their ankles. Their naked bodies entwined, they explored each other thoroughly. Grief is a powerful bond. Ethan felt sensations he had never felt before in his life. He experienced the most intimate thing that seemed possible between two human beings. They never left the hotel room and the passion continued on for hours until they snuggled up under the covers, exhausted, spooning each other, Ethan gently clutching Travis's chest. They slept like that for the rest of the night.

Daylight and loud rapping woke them up. The sun peeked around the window shade, and somebody was speaking.

"Travis! Ethan! Are you in there?" It was the booming voice of Mr. Bennet. "What the hell's goin' on with you two? We're all set to move out! You're keeping us waiting!"

"Holy shit!" Travis said, and they both jumped out of bed and scrambled for their clothes.

"What time is it?"

Travis, still naked, fumbled for his pocket watch. "Eight-thirty!" He said in a louder voice, "Sorry, Mr. Bennet, I'm afraid we overslept. We'll be right out." They sorted out the jumble of clothing on the floor and dressed quickly.

When they rejoined the troupe, they found everyone in better spirits. The men had all bathed and shaved and eaten a good hearty breakfast, and were ready to set out. Ethan and Travis were the only ones who were still disheveled.

As the herd moved out, everything seemed to be back to normal. Ethan rode alone in the rear. No one was interested in taking Josh's place.

*   *   *

One night after supper, the men sat on boulders around a campfire drinking a stale pot of coffee. Fred, Don and Joe had been not-so-secretly topping up their cups from a large bottle of recently acquired corn whiskey. The only one who didn't know about it was Mr. Bennet, and no one was interested in ratting them out. After Mr. Bennet turned in for the night, they brought the bottle out into the open, though most of the others just ignored them, basking in the warmth of the fire and Virgil's mournful music. Since Josh's death, Virgil had played nothing but melancholy songs.

"Hey!" Fred kicked a log into the fire, sending a spray of sparks at Virgil. "Either play something fast or shut that thing up!" His speech was slurred. Virgil chose to shut the thing up.

The three of them continued to get more and more inebriated and the more they drank, the more menacing they became.

Don eyed Ethan. "Hey you! Book boy!" he snarled. "Why don't you tell us a story? Something romantic, with some fairies!" The three of them burst into laughter. Travis glared at them but said nothing. Ethan dropped his gaze to the ground and said nothing.

"Here, puss, puss." Fred said smacking his lips at Ethan. Another outburst of laughter. "I'll bet your lily white fingers have never even fired a gun. You know you ain't no kitty cat. Yer just a goddamn little filly!"

"That's enough!" Travis jumped up and faced Fred. "I'm warning you to leave him alone!"

"What're you protectin' him for? You his *wet-nurse* or somethin'?"

Travis's fist connected with Fred's left cheekbone. Don and Joe jumped on Travis and began hammering him in the face and gut. It was happening so fast, Ethan just sat frozen – then, realizing his beloved was being pummeled, leapt onto Don's back, wrapped his arm around his neck in a choke hold and squeezed with all his might. Don stopped punching Travis and tried to get Ethan off his back, scrabbling at Ethan's arm, face turning blue. Meanwhile, Virgil and Patrick restrained Joe. Fred was still sitting on the ground, dazed. Mr. Bennet charged out of his tent.

"What the hell's goin' on out here? Why aren't you jackasses in bed?" He surveyed the situation. Travis was bent over gasping for air, cheek bruised and nose trickling blood. Ethan had released Don, who was heaving for air himself. The half-empty bottle lay on its side by Fred's foot. Bennet picked it up.

"God damn it!" He hurled it into the fire. The glass smashed on the logs and the fire erupted to five times its normal size. "We're already behind schedule. And now I find you all drunk and brawlin'. I have half a mind to dock the whole lot of you a full day's pay! Now who started it?"

"I did, sir," Travis said.

"Travis? You?" Mr. Bennet looked surprised and suspicious.

"Yes sir. I threw the first punch. You can ask any of the guys."

"It was him done it all right," Joe said. Fred and Don, drunk and guilty as sin, nodded.

"All right," Bennet said. "Who's on guard duty?"

David stepped forward. He had been with the cows when the fight started but had run back to camp to see what the ruckus was about.

"David, you're relieved. I want everyone in bed now. We've got an early start in the morning. Travis has got guard duty for the rest of the night."

They all went into their tents, Ethan included. But Ethan didn't go to bed. He sat in his tent and waited until it got quiet and all the cowboys were asleep, then he quietly left his tent to join Travis. He found him sitting at the base of a tree overlooking the herd.

"Ethan, you should be sleeping." His nose had stopped bleeding and a nasty purple bruise darkened his left cheek.

"I had to know if you were okay."

Travis put his hand to his side. "I'm a little sore in the ribs, but I'll mend."

"How come you took the blame?"

"Trust me, it's easier that way. Those three are already enough trouble without getting them riled up more."

"I can't believe you punched him. I didn't know you were a fighter."

"I'm not. I've never been a brawler. But when they started in on you like that, I just couldn't help myself. I had to do something. So I did. I didn't even think about it. It just kind of came out of nowhere."

Ethan studied the purple cheek for a moment. "Thank you."

"Same here." Travis chuckled, his hand went to his sore ribs. "I saw what you did to Don."

Ethan smiled, and was glad it was too dark for Travis to see his red face.

"I'd never been in a fight before in my life. When I was in school, a lot of the boys used to pick on me because I was quiet and odd. They would have beat me up if they could, but I could always outrun them. So I was never in a fight because I always ran away." As Ethan sat on the ground facing Travis, he absent-mindedly fingered a twig. He was thinking over all his childhood memories. After a few minutes he continued. "Willie was different though. He never ran away from a fight in his life. Heck, He even started a few. And if Willie was around when any of the guys were picking on me, I wouldn't have to run away either, 'cause Willie would take care of them. He'd fight for me. You think I'm a coward, Travis?"

"Of course not. You were just smart enough to keep yourself from getting hurt. A coward is someone who runs away when somebody else is being hurt. And you proved tonight that you're no coward."

"But that's just because it was you being hurt. A year ago, I probably would have just stood and watched."

"Maybe, or maybe not. We never really know until we're in that position."

"Did boys pick on you when you were in school?"

"Not much. I was probably in a few schoolyard fights, but I don't have any clear memory of it."

"How could you not remember being in fights?"

"I don't know. I just blocked it out. There's a lot I don't remember about my childhood. I know as a man, I've only been in one other fight in my life and that was with my father."

Ethan's eyes went wide. "You fought with your father?"

"Well, first of all you've got to understand that my father was a very religious man, and he had very little use for anyone who didn't take to his religion. He was going to bring up all his children to be God-fearing Christians even if he had to beat it into them. And he did too. One of his favorite bible quotes was 'spare the rod – spoil the child.' Well, I was just about the age you are now, maybe a little older. We were all sitting at the supper table having a conversation and I made a comment about something. I don't even remember what it was, but my father didn't like it one bit. He said something about it being blasphemous and he wouldn't have that kind of talk in his house. Well that's when I got a little huffy and said I was a man now and entitled to my own opinions. I can tell you he would have none of that. He got up and grabbed the strap that hung on the wall and meant to whip the fear of God into my soul, right in front of my little sisters. I can remember exactly what I said to him. 'You just try it old man, and it will be the last thing you do.' Well, you can bet that set him off. I went out the door, he came after me and we slugged it out in front of the house."

Ethan sat, mouth open. His own father had a pretty mean spirit, but he had never beaten his sons.

"It wasn't long after that I left home to start working as a ranch hand."

There was a new moon, and clouds moved in to obscure the stars so that the sky was dark as blackberry jam. The only noise was the chirping crickets. Ethan reached over and held Travis's hand.

"Go ahead and lay back and rest for a while. I'll watch the cows, Travis."

Chapter Twelve

As August waned, the trail to Cheyenne took them through Colorado Springs and past Denver. The weather had held up, and they traveled in only a few days of rain. This was the final leg, and there would be no more towns before Cheyenne.

One clear day, as the sun illuminated every stone and crevice of the Rockies in the west, Travis retreated from his position in the herd to meet up with Ethan.

"Come on, follow me. I've got something to show you."

"Right now? We can't leave the herd."

"The cows can get by without us for a little while."

As they started to gallop away, Ethan looked over at Virgil, who was frowning. They galloped in the same direction as the herd, quickly passing it by and drawing the attention of every man on the drive. As they left the herd behind, Mr. Bennet yelled out.

"Hey! Just where the hell do you think you're going?"

"We won't be gone long!"

"TRAVIS GET BACK HERE RIGHT NOW! GODDAMIT YOU'RE NOT BEING PAID TO GO SIGHT SEEING!"

They ignored his ravings and kept right on going. Travis knew exactly where he was going: a large and long valley. Cliffs cut along the valley on one side, and Travis led Ethan up its face on a rocky path. It was a steep climb for the horses, but eventually they made their way to the top of the bluff.

Laid out before them was the vast, grassy valley. From this height it looked as deep as a canyon. The wind rippled through the grass and transformed it to a great, green body of water. Ethan stood up in his stirrups and inhaled deeply; the wind rushed through his body. The aroma of pine and fresh earth filled him. All that mattered was the future.

"Travis, what's going to happen to us after the cattle drive is over?" There. He had said it.

"What would you like to happen?"

"I want us to be together. I don't want to lose you."

"There's no reason you have to. To tell you the truth I've been giving it a lot of thought myself."

"Really?"

"You know how I told you I wanted to build a horse ranch? Well, why don't we do it together? We could come back right here, to Colorado, just the two of us, build it together and spend the rest of our days, raising horses. It could be a real good life."

Ethan noticed that way off to the right, the herd was just beginning to funnel into the valley below them.

"Would we come here straight away? I mean as soon as the drive is over?"

"Well, no. I think first we need to go back to Texas and settle our affairs. Don't you? I mean it would only be fair to at least go and say goodbye to our families. After all, your mother is waiting for you. Think how she would feel if you never came back."

The thought of his mother gave Ethan a pang. He preferred to write her a letter, but he knew that Travis was right. He had to go home and face her.

"Building a ranch is going to take some time," Travis said. "We'll have to find some small place to live first. And we'll have to find work. Denver's a good place to start. Have you ever been to Denver, Ethan? What am I thinking? Of course you haven't. You've never been anywhere. Anyway, there's a lot going on in Denver. It's just west of here, and there's lots of work. They have sawmills, and sheep ranches and mining. It shouldn't be hard to find a little homestead for a really low price.

On the way back we can pass through it, you know, nose around and see what prospects there are. Maybe we can even find a place and go ahead and buy it with our pay from the cattle drive. What do you think?"

Ethan took off his hat, ran his fingers through his hair, and relished the wind on his scalp. "I can't tell you how happy I am right now."

Travis had to give a little smile. Down below the herd had completely flooded the valley. They sat quietly on their horses and watched the herd pass.

"My mother is not going to like the news," Ethan said.

"I know." Travis leaned over rubbed Cleo's shoulder to soothe her jitteriness. "She didn't like the idea of you coming on this cattle drive either. But she accepted it. She'll adjust to this too. She knows that she can't keep you sitting on her lap forever."

"So what exactly do we want to do when we go back to Texas?"

Cleo raked the ground with her hoof, ready to go. Travis tightened the reins. "I thought we'd go to your place first and settle things with your family. We can buy a wagon to carry whatever things you want to bring along. We can stay for about a week, then go to San Antone and see my folks. We'll pick up my stuff and then be on our way."

"What are we going to tell everybody? I mean about what we're doing?"

He gave Cleo her head and she turned around in a circle. "We'll simply tell them the truth. We've decided to go into business together as horse breeders and we're going to build a horse ranch in Colorado. Men start business partnerships all the time."

The herd had now completely passed through the valley and was starting to vanish from view.

"We had better be getting back," Travis said. "Bennet's going to be mad as a hornet."

Thinking of home, Ethan's conscience prickled. He had come on the cattle drive to help his mother in case Willie failed, and now he was planning to abandon her. He buried that thought for later. His head was spinning and his limbs buzzed with energy. He tore off his hat, waved it high in the air and yelled out the loudest cowboy "Yahoo!" that had ever echoed in the valley.

They carefully descended the cliff into the valley and raced off to rejoin the herd from the rear. It didn't take them long to catch up, and Virgil was startled when they came upon him unawares. Ethan slipped back into his normal position and Travis went on ahead.

"What in tarnation have you two been up to?" Virgil asked. "You've been gone for darn near an hour!"

"Just seeing the sights," Ethan replied. Up ahead he could hear Mr. Bennet bellowing. Poor Travis was getting an earful.

Chapter Thirteen

Once another dusty little town, it was a hub for beef distribution, and Cheyenne was devoid of any color but brown; every green growing thing had been stamped out by foot traffic, and the place stank of tanning hides and manure. The well trod cattle-trail ended in a wide berth at the train station located on the outskirts of town. The trains carried livestock all the way to Chicago in the east and all the way to San Francisco in the west. There was a rectangular layout of corrals divided into three large sections, all made of wooden planks that were weathered and warped, so big it could accommodate at least three large herds. Adjoining were smaller corrals for horses and other livestock. A series of chutes led from the corrals to ramps that went right up to the train tracks, and the cattle buyers' offices were adjacent to the train station.

They rolled into Cheyenne, the first week of September, only a week behind Mr. Bennet's schedule. As the herd funneled through the gates into the corral, auditors from the buyers began to tag and count the cows. There was in excess of eleven hundred. Mr. Bennet entered the cattle buyers' office to handle the negotiations and transactions. After the last of the herd was through the gates, the cowboys jumped down off their horses, secured them to the hitching posts and each found a section of fence to hop up on or lean against. Their job was done. While they waited for their pay, they watched the trains roll in and the workers load freight onto the cars.

Ethan sat on top of the rickety corral and Travis stood beside him, back to the corral and elbows on the top rail. Word was just beginning to spread through town that the overdue herd had finally arrived. Betsy had obviously not heard yet, because she was nowhere to be seen. Ethan observed the city folk. They were much like the people in his own hometown only more of them. Women in hoopskirts and puffy sleeves walked down the wooden plank sidewalks carrying baskets. Young boys played in the streets wearing cowboy hats and pretending to shoot each other with carved wooden guns. Horse drawn wagons pulled up to the train station to pick up merchandise that had been delivered. Forty-five minutes later, Mr. Bennet stepped out of the office and motioned for the men to come in.

"Yee-hah!" David yelled. "It's time to get our pay!" They pressed into the office; there was a small desk right inside the door with a roster and a briefcase full of money. Mr. Bennet sat behind the desk and the cowboys stood in line and one by one collected their cash and signed their name on the roster. While Ethan was waiting behind Travis in line, he was looking out of the dirty windows when he saw a young woman in a green floral dress and a bonnet walk by, looking around as if searching. Virgil spotted her too.

"It's my Betsy!" he cried and forfeited his place in line to greet her. Through the window Ethan saw him run up behind her. She turned and threw her arms around him. They embraced one another and kissed. Virgil was so happy to see her he lifted her right off the ground. She really didn't look anything like Ethan had expected – short and somewhat homely with fair skin, buck teeth and brown curls peeking out from underneath her bonnet. They hugged, then talked, then hugged some more, then kissed again, and talked some more.

Travis had just pocketed his money and signed the roster.

"Ethan, the Haywood Ranch would like to thank you for your service," Mr. Bennet said in an unfamiliar, professional tone. He counted out Ethan's money, and asked him to sign his name. Ethan did so and then began counting his money for himself.

"It's all there," Mr. Bennet laughed. "Your service is now complete. Please surrender your horse to Bunny over at the horse corral." He shook Ethan's hand and sent him on his way.

Outside the cowboys gathered around Virgil and Betsy.

"Hey everybody, Betsy and me are gettin' married tomorrow morning and we want y'all to come!"

"Under one condition," Patrick said.

"What's that?"

"That you let us all take you out drinkin' tonight!"

"You've got a deal."

They all laughed and slapped Virgil on the back, and as a group they all made their way into town.

"Don't you want to go drinking with the guys?" Ethan asked.

"Come on Ethan, you know me better than that." Travis stepped closer, and faced Ethan with smiling eyes. "I've got other plans for us tonight. I know of this great little Italian restaurant in town. We can spend some of this money on good food, and do some shopping. I'll bet you'd like to get some presents for your mother and Miss Peet wouldn't you?" He put his hand on Ethan's shoulder and leaned in with his mouth almost touching Ethan's ear. "And then we can get the nicest hotel room in town and celebrate our own way."

They led their horses over to the supply wagon, which was parked next to a small corral with three horses inside. Bunny was leaning up against the wagon taking little nips from his whisky bottle. He nodded to Ethan and Travis and pulled open the gate to the corral. Ethan led his horse in.

"So long old boy." Ethan stroked the horse's nose. The horse snorted and stamped his foot, seeming to understand that he was being parted from another rider as he had been in many cattle drives before. Travis got up onto Cleo and held out his hand to Ethan.

"Come on, let's go."

Ethan took his hand and swung up into the saddle behind him, and they rode into town. They left the stinking shipping yards behind and passed the outdoor farmers' markets into the main drag of town. Virgil passed them as he was walking back to the cattle buyers' office.

"Forgot to get my pay," he said sheepishly.

The Third Part:
San Antone

Chapter One

Just as the sun touched the horizon, Ethan and Travis, riding on Cleo, rounded the bend that concealed the Keller boarding house. This final day of their two and a half week journey back home had been a long and tedious one. They were both dog-tired and looking forward to sleeping in real beds that night. Ethan had ridden behind Travis for the whole journey, and while he appreciated the intimacy, he was glad it was almost over. They had traveled fifty to sixty miles a day and had camped out under the stars almost every night. The homestead looked exactly the same as Ethan remembered it. But somehow it seemed like somebody else's home, undoubtedly because he knew he would be leaving. They had only been gone for three and a half months, but it could have been three and a half years. Willie was working in the field, a lone figure digging up potatoes. As they rode up to the homestead, he came in from the field to greet them.

"Hey little brother! It's about time you got back. Ma's been watching out the window for you for the past two weeks! Now maybe she'll relax and stop worrying."

They dismounted Cleo and stretched their legs. Travis greeted Willie, who nodded politely. Ethan emptied the contents of the saddlebags into a burlap sack and Travis led Cleo to the water trough and wrapped the reins around the hitching post. As the three of them walked up onto the porch, Ethan noticed that the loose rail had been secured and painted. He felt a little queasy knowing he was about to see his mother again, but as a changed man. He had no money to offer her. They entered the parlor, Ophelia looked up from her sewing, stared at them for a moment as though her eyes might be playing a trick on her, and then a smile bloomed on her lips. She threw aside her sewing, jumped up, grabbed Ethan, kissed him on the cheek and hugged him tightly. Travis hung back, watching.

"Oh thank God you're finally back! I'm so happy! I haven't received any letters from you in weeks and I was beginning to think that something terrible had happened to you! Oh dear, you look exhausted! And you're so thin. I knew you wouldn't be able to get enough to eat!" Ophelia had just noticed Travis's presence. "Oh, hello. It's so nice to see you again."

"Yes ma'am." Travis removed his hat and nodded.

"I brought you something from Cheyenne," Ethan said reaching into the burlap sack and pulling out a folded lace tablecloth.

"Oh, Ethan it's just lovely! I've never seen such fine work." She ran her fingers over the intricate pattern. "I will only use this on the most special occasions. You must both tell me all about the cattle drive, but you must be famished. I'll start cooking supper immediately. Travis, I insist you stay and join us for supper."

"Thank you, ma'am."

"Just sit yourselves down and relax and I'll have supper ready in just a bit." She bustled off into the kitchen. While they waited for supper, the three of them sat down in the parlor, Ethan and Travis on the sofa, Willie on the chair across from them, leaning over with his forearms on his knees, hands dangling in between. His knuckles were cut up and bruised.

"So how'd it go? Anything exciting happen?"

"We saw a lot of different looking country," Ethan answered.

"That's not what I mean. Was there like any Indian raids, or gun fighting, or rustling?"

"Not at all." Travis shrugged, "Everything went smooth as silk. Other than a few minor injuries and, well..." His eyes dropped to the floor. Ethan knew he was thinking of Josh but didn't want to bring it up.

"Too bad. It sounds pretty boring if you ask me."

"It wasn't boring," Ethan said. "It was the most exciting time of my life. We had to brave the elements. We almost didn't make it across the desert, and then we had to get through the storms, and climb up into the mountains."

Willie just shook his head and rolled his eyes. He wasn't impressed. They sat for a few minutes in awkward silence, then Willie leaned toward Ethan and lowered his voice so that their mother wouldn't hear. "But I'll bet you had yourself some fine whores in the towns you passed through, didn't you little brother?"

Ethan stared at the floor and didn't answer.

"He did okay," Travis answered. "He got his fair share." Ethan faked a smile and Willie beamed with pride thinking he had broken his brother in. Not finding anything more worthwhile to discuss, he excused himself to go and get cleaned up for supper.

"Do you think we should tell them about Josh?" Ethan asked once they were alone.

Travis shook his head. "They didn't know him. It won't do any good to upset your mother, thinking how it could have been you instead of Josh. Besides, she's going to be upset enough as it is when you tell her we're leaving."

True to form, Ophelia had supper ready in forty-five minutes. Ophelia was a woman of such extreme organization that she always had the day's meals planned in advance and did a lot of the preparation earlier in the day – skinning and cutting up the chicken, removing the peas from their pods, cutting up the vegetables – so that when she went into the kitchen to prepare the meal, she was just putting on some finishing touches, making the biscuits, and sticking everything in the oven, but her guests thought she was simply a marvel in the kitchen.

"Where are Mr. Ponce, Mr. Baker, and Mr. Pendegast?" he inquired.

"Mr. Pendegast is probably still at the bank," Ophelia said as they all took their seats around the table. A feast was set before them of chicken stew, hot biscuits with butter, sweet peas, carrots glazed with brown sugar, and cranberries. "As for the other two, I'm afraid they have moved out."

"Why? What happened?"

She gave a sharp look at Willie. "Apparently they weren't getting along with your brother. I've put up a notice in the general store. Hopefully we'll be able to replace them."

"Ma, I told you I'll find you some new boarders!" Willie ladled out a large helping of chicken stew into his bowl.

"Ethan, now that you're home, Mr. Simpson can give you back your job. The new boy he hired will be quite disappointed, but after all, he knew it was only temporary."

Ethan didn't want to disrupt supper with the bad news. During the meal they talked about everything that had happened on the cattle drive and Ethan gave his mother vivid descriptions of the landscapes, the mountains, and the towns. They talked briefly about the thunderstorm and even more briefly about Ethan's injury. Nobody mentioned Josh or his fate.

They were just finishing the last of the meal when Ophelia asked, "So what are your plans now, Travis? Are you going to move on to another cattle drive, or are you going to stick around here for a while?"

"Ma, actually I have something to discuss with you about that," Ethan said.

"Oh? What is it?" She raised her brows and met Ethan's eyes, unflinching.

"Ma'am if you'll excuse me, I promised a drink to a friend in town," Travis said folding his napkin and scooting his chair back.

"But Travis, you haven't had any dessert yet."

"No thank you, ma'am. I'm sorry I have to run off like this. I'll see you tomorrow, Ethan." And with that he grabbed his hat, nodded to Ophelia, and was out the door. Willie frowned.

"Now I wonder what was so important that he had to run off all of a sudden like that?" Willie mused.

"Ma, I have something very important to tell you." His gut tightened and he had to concentrate to keep his voice from wavering.

"What is it, dear?" She stood up and began gathering up the dishes.

He took a breath, clinched his fist, and spit it out. "Travis and I are going to Colorado."

She stopped what she was doing and sat back down. "What? Whatever for? You just came from there. Why do you need to go back there?"

"We're going there for good, Ma. We're going to build a horse ranch and breed horses."

Her mouth dropped open like she was about to say something, then she closed it again. After thinking for a moment she said, "Okay. I'm sure that in a few years…"

"No, Ma. I mean now. We're leaving in a week."

"Ethan you can't! You're only seventeen! You're way too young to be going off on your own!" She wrung her hands, her brow furrowed, looking like she wanted to give up and die on the spot.

"I knew you were going to be like this. I know you're upset, but it's all settled. We've already bought a little house in Denver with our money from the cattle drive."

"Oh no! Ethan! Why do you do this to your poor mother? You've only just got home and now you tell me you're leaving again in a week? You can't do this Ethan. I won't let you. Tell him Willie. Tell him he's too young to leave home!"

Willie had been listening to this whole exchange with amusement. He pushed back from the table with exaggerated precision.

"Well, Ma. It looks to me like my little brother's made up his mind. You best be helping him pack his things and wishing him good luck."

"Willie!"

"It won't do you no good to fuss over it, Ma. Your fussin' didn't stop him from going on the cattle drive, and it's not gonna stop him from doing this either. Congratulations, little brother, it looks like you'll be the first one to break free of this place. You're leaving in a week, you say?"

Ethan had to swallow the lump in his throat to answer normally. "Yep. First we're going to San Antonio to see Travis's family and say goodbye to them. We'll stay there another week and then hcad off to Denver."

"Why do you have to go with Travis to San Antonio?" Ophelia asked. "Why do you have to be with him when he goes to see *his* family? Can't you stay here and meet up with him later? It'll give us more time together. Ethan, please stay longer. I'm not ready to have you leave again."

"Ma, please. We've already got it planned out."

"Whatever am I going to do without my boy?" she cried, putting her hands up to her mouth.

"I'll still come back and visit sometimes."

"I knew you'd leave someday, I just didn't think it would be so soon!" Her voice muffled, she wouldn't meet his eyes, but stared with a vacant look.

Ethan had no immunity against the guilt she gave him. Her reaction was almost exactly as he had imagined it would be. Now he watched her as she turned away and began to clear away the dirty dishes from the table. All her joy had turned to sorrow, and it gnawed at his gut. He knew there was nothing he could do or say that would make her feel any different now.

"I'm really beat, Ma. If you don't mind, I think I'll go to bed now."

She stifled a whimper and shooed him. He went into his bedroom, which was exactly as he had left it, and closed the door. He pulled off his boots, undressed, and flung himself down on the bed, with his face buried in the pillow so Willie couldn't here him as he cried himself to sleep.

Chapter Two

Around three o'clock the next afternoon, Ethan loitered outside the schoolhouse. While he waited he sat down on an old barrel in front of the sawmill across the street. The little schoolhouse was slightly larger than when he had attended, but he remembered being the last student to leave every day, usually with his nose stuck in a book. His mother had improved slightly by morning. Her despair had mellowed into depression, and a huge breakfast was waiting for him when he got up. But she had little to say to him, and he had come into town to see if he could kill some time until school let out. He stopped over at the livery stable to see the horses, then wandered around town peeking in shop windows, watching the lumberjacks load wood onto the wagons, more to the point, he just did nothing. Once he had situated himself across from the schoolhouse, he found that he didn't have long to wait. The door banged open and thirty children came pouring out like inmates out of prison. The younger children ran and jumped and tagged each other, and the older girls flocked together to trade gossip on their route home. After all the students had dissipated, Ethan crossed the street. He entered the schoolroom quietly; Miss Peet looked up from the papers she was grading.

"Ethan!" She jumped up to give him a quick little hug that was just long enough to remain within the realm of propriety. "Oh, you must have so much to tell me. The last letter I received said you were just about to arrive in Cheyenne. Sit down and tell me everything." Her eyes shining, and her voice higher and sweeter – so different from when she taught him.

"I got this for you while I was in Cheyenne," he said, pulling a book out of his leather satchel. "It's a first edition of *Twenty Thousand Leagues Under The Sea.*"

"Thank you so much, Ethan." She took the book and fanned the pages. "You shouldn't have. This must have been very expensive. It's leather bound and in near perfect condition." She closed it and held it against her bosom. "But thank you, it will be a proud addition to my library."

Miss Peet gently placed the book on top of her desk like it was a delicate artifact and sat back down in her chair. Ethan sat down on top of the student desk closest to her. She asked all sorts of questions about the cattle drive and the towns. He went into meticulous detail, and covered the whole experience from start to finish, even about Josh's death. He only omitted one thing – his relationship with Travis. He ached to be able to share it with her, and somehow his exuberant feelings betrayed him.

"Ethan, there's something different about you. I can't put my finger on it, but somehow you're changed."

Ethan shrugged; he didn't know how to hide it.

"It's like there's a glow about you. If I didn't know better, I would almost say you were in love."

Ethan's heart pounded in his chest. His cheeks flushed and he felt a little dizzy.

"Oh! That's it, isn't it? Ethan you're in love!"

No use denying it. "Yes, Miss Peet. As a matter of fact I am."

"This is so wonderful! You must tell me everything about her at once! Did you meet her in one of the towns on the trail?"

"No. That's not quite it."

"She's a girl from here in town then?"

Miss Peet was bound to worm out every last detail. "No."

"Well who is she and where did you meet her?"

He must be careful. "I can't tell you that."

"Why not? Oh." She broke into a secretive smile. "I understand. She doesn't know how you feel about her."

A little information might not hurt. "That's not it either. We are very much in love with each other. But you'll just have to trust me that I can't tell you anything more."

Miss Peet slapped her hands on her knees. "Oh, this won't do at all! I simply must know who she is. The curiosity will eat me alive."

The corners of his mouth slightly went up as he tried to suppress his smile. "I really wish I could tell you."

"Well then, out with it. I'm going to find out eventually anyway, if you two are going to be married."

"It's more complicated than that."

"Ethan, please tell me. I can't stand it any longer. Who is she?"

He hesitated, his heart sped up, and he tossed away his defenses. "Okay I'll tell you. But you must swear to me that you will never tell another living soul about it."

Miss Peet's smile faded over this complication. "Why? I don't understand why you need to be so secretive."

"You'll understand when I tell you, but I won't tell you unless you swear to it."

Miss Peet's smile returned. She was happy just to have her curiosity sated – very much like a child. "Okay, okay. I swear I will never tell another living soul."

"All right then." Ethan's hands began to tremble and a nervous laugh escaped him. "Brace yourself. The person I'm in love with is not a girl at all. It's a man – Travis Cain."

Miss Peet sat speechless for a long time. Then her confusion shattered and she burst out laughing.

"Oh Ethan. You really had me fooled there for a minute! You are such a funny, funny boy. You're poking fun at me because you knew that I had designs on Travis." She continued laughing, her face was crimson.

"No, Miss Peet. It's not a joke. I'm being very serious." Ethan began to feel a little queasy in his stomach. "Travis and I are in love. In fact we bought a small house in Denver and we're moving there in about a week. That's the main thing I came to tell you."

Her laughing slowly wilted. "Oh my God. Ethan you *are*

serious." The stupefied look returned to her face.

"Yes. It's absolutely true. We're moving to Denver where we're going to start building a ranch and we're going to breed horses. But as far as everyone else is concerned we're just business partners. You understand now why I swore you to secrecy?"

"Yes of course." She began to shuffle the papers on her desk. "Ethan, if you don't mind could we *not* talk about this? I really think it's better if we just pretend we never had this conversation."

"Well, okay." Ethan was disappointed. Somehow he had the idea that Miss Peet would be happy for him. "But you did swear. You won't tell anybody."

"Of course not." Miss Peet would no longer make eye contact with him. "I do appreciate the book. It's one of the few first editions I now own. I always take very good care of those because of their value. I never even loan them out."

"I'm leaving town next Friday morning." Ethan stood, picked up his satchel and nervously rubbed the leather between his fingers. "You *will* come to see me off, Miss Peet?"

"Yes I'll come. Ethan, if you don't mind, I've had a headache all day, and I really need to finish grading these papers so I can get home and go to bed. You understand."

"Of course Miss Peet." Ethan picked up his satchel, slowly turned towards the door, and looked back over his shoulder. "I'll see you Friday then?"

She did not look up from her gradebook. "Yes Ethan. Bye."

*   *   *

From the schoolhouse Ethan went to the hotel. He went up to the front desk and interrupted a clerk's game of solitaire.

"Excuse me, sir. Could you tell me what room Travis Cain is in?"

The clerk, with his starched collar, high forehead and slicked-back hair, had a foreboding look about him. Ethan had never had reason to go into the hotel before, and he was a stranger to the clerk. He laid down his cards, looked Ethan up and down as though he were trying to ascertain whether or not Ethan might be a nuisance to his guest, and then scanned the register with his finger stopping at Travis's name.

"Yes. He's in room seven."

"Thank you." Ethan trotted up the stairs and knocked on the door to room seven. Travis let him in, setting aside a pair of boots and a rag. After closing the door, Ethan threw his arms around Travis and wrapped his legs around his waist so that Travis was holding him up off the floor. Ethan broke into laughter and kissed him.

"I missed you last night," Ethan said. "I hate sleeping alone."

"Me too. How'd it go with your mother?"

Ethan uncoiled his legs and stepped back. "As expected. She started having fits. But it's all settled now. I can't wait until we get to Denver.

Travis picked up the rag and went back to cleaning his boots. "It won't be long now. We still have to take care of my family and then we'll be all set."

Ethan thought about telling Travis about his conversation with Miss Peet, but then decided against it. He was afraid Travis might think he had been a fool.

Chapter Three

By Friday morning Travis had purchased a covered wagon secondhand from Deputy Sloan, and loaded up all of Ethan's belongings. Cleo was hitched and they were ready to set out, and Travis, Ethan, Willie, and Ophelia stood by the wagon saying their goodbyes. Miss Peet had not come to see him off. He kept glancing up the road and didn't hear his mother's question. Maybe Miss Peet just needed time to adjust to the idea and everything would be okay.

"How long is it going to take you to get there?" Ophelia asked.

"We should arrive somewhere around suppertime tonight," Travis replied.

Ophelia wiped away her tears with her handkerchief. "I just wish we had more time."

Willie patted his brother on the back. "Good luck, little brother. Who knows? Maybe I'll be passing through Denver sometime and I'll see you."

"Thanks, Willie." They shook hands. Ethan turned to face his mother. She hugged him and held him tight and sobbed.

"Ma, please," he said helplessly.

"I'm gonna miss you so much. My baby's all grown up and leaving me." In between sobs she managed to give out instructions. Write me every week. Get plenty to eat. Take care of yourself. And so on. She finally let him go and they climbed up onto the buckboard. Travis took the reins and gave a cluck, at which Cleo bobbed her head and heaved the wagon forward. As they slowly rolled away, gaining momentum, Ethan looked back to see his mother waving her handkerchief. He waved and watched her recede; she cried so hard she turned to Willie for comfort. He put his arms around her while she cried into his chest. Ethan was surprised that Willie was actually capable of showing compassion.

*　　　*　　　*

Around four-thirty they turned up the path to the Cain homestead. It was not at all what Ethan was expecting. Where he had imagined something like his own homestead or even larger and more luxurious, it was just a simple farmhouse, slightly run down but functional enough. There was a lofty barn that was as weather beaten as the house, and a small grove of trees to the east. All around were fallow fields and dry sagebrush. As they climbed down off the wagon, Travis's mother and three young sisters came running out of the house, shrieking with delight. Travis jumped down just as they came up to the wagon.

"Travis, what a surprise! I can't believe you're really here!" Mrs. Cain caught her son in her arms and squeezed so hard her ropy forearms shook.

"They didn't know you were coming?" Ethan asked.

"Travis ain't one for writin'," she said. "It's always a surprise when he shows up." Mrs. Cain was a handsome, proud woman. She was more elegant than his own mother, but not as refined as Miss Peet. Her dress was simple yet flattering, free of hoops or bustles, its lone ornament a high collar that suited her long neck. She had beautiful auburn hair that hung to her elbows, unbound and parted in the center.

Travis hugged each one of his sisters. The three girls crowded around him; the two younger ones jumping and dancing, the older one hovering with a shy smile.

"Mother I would like you to meet my friend, Ethan Keller. He and I were on a cattle drive together and we became good friends. And Ethan, these are my sisters Eva, she's fourteen,

Jane, she's ten, and Katie here is seven." Ethan bowed to each of them. When he came to Eva, she blushed and shyly dropped her eyes to the ground. She was closest to Ethan's age and he recognized that way that girls got when they were attracted to him. She was a smaller version of her mother, only with long blonde hair.

"I've got presents for everybody!" Travis said in a teasing way. Katie and Jane cheered and jumped up and down. He pulled a sack out of the wagon, opened it up, looked inside, and made a face. "Ah, you don't want these old presents, I'll just take them to the orphanage."

"Oh yes we do! Please! We really want them!" Katie wasn't sure if he was teasing or not.

"Oh, okay then." The group moved to the porch where he pulled a doll out of the sack and handed it to Katie. He gave Jane a stereoscope, and Eva a locket. The three girls thanked him profusely and admired their gifts. For his mother, out of the sack he pulled a fox-fur stole.

"Travis! It's beautiful. You are the best son a mother could ever have. Thank you, dear."

Travis tossed the empty sack aside, and allowed his gaze to roam around the property. "Where's father?"

"He's still at the shop working. He should be home around six o'clock. How long are you going to stay this time?"

"For a week."

Mrs. Cain took her son by the arm. "Let's go inside and I'll cook y'all a big supper. After all, this is a special occasion."

Ethan followed them into the house trailing by several yards. He felt like an interloper in their family reunion.

"You two boys just sit down and rest yourselves while I get started cooking," Mrs. Cain instructed. Ethan and Travis sat down in two hard chairs opposite the fireplace. In the parlor were two more chairs and the dining table. The kitchen was a small room adjacent to it and there were three bedrooms just off the opposite end. The larger bedroom was for Mr. and Mrs. Cain and the smaller bedrooms were for the girls, with Jane and Katie sharing one. Checkered curtains hung in the windows and a large round woven rug covered the rough wood floor and smelled faintly of dog. Hanging on the unfinished wood walls were a few framed tintypes of solemn ancestors. Mrs. Cain stepped out of the kitchen and summoned Eva and Jane to come help her. Jane dragged her feet and whined, still looking at the pictures through her stereoscope, but Katie gave her a swat and went back to setting up new quarters for her doll in the corner of the parlor.

Mrs. Cain would pop her head out of the kitchen door every once in a while to ask a question or comment on some recent bit of hometown news. It was through this style of communication that she found out where Ethan lived and how old he was and what his interests were. She also made the comment that she thought it was awfully nice of Ethan to accompany Travis home for this visit. Her hospitality towards him was so sincere that Ethan felt she really did want him there. Soon he was laughing and Travis was crawling around on the floor giving Katie horseback rides.

The mantle clock chimed six o'clock, and Mrs. Cain set the last tureen and plate of supper. Jane had gone back to looking at her stereoscope and Eva shyly sat in the corner of the room, trying not to let Ethan catch her looking at him. Outside, the sound of boots stomped up the porch steps and the door banged open. Mr. Cain entered the room and his mouth fell open at the sight of his son. Travis took after his father; they had the same lean frame and tanned skin. Mr. Cain was basically just an older, more weathered version of Travis.

He gave Travis a one-armed hug. "It's good to see you, son," he said and looked in Ethan's direction with no discernable expression on his face.

"Father, this is Ethan Keller. He's a friend of mine."

Ethan extended his hand. "Pleasure to meet you, sir."

"Likewise." He shook Ethan's hand then turned to his wife. "Well Catherine, what have you cooked us for supper?"

They all sat down around the dinner table, which was much too small to accommodate seven people and a feast. Mr. Cain sat at the head of the table with Mrs. Cain sitting opposite, Eva and Jane on one side, and Travis, Ethan and Katie all bunched up on the other. As they were short one chair, Katie sat on a soap box. When they were settled, everyone grew still in their chairs.

Ethan wondered what they were waiting for. Mr. Cain bowed his head and everyone else followed his lead and bowed their heads, too. Ethan felt a little peculiar, but tilted his face down and stared at his lap.

Mr. Cain prayed in a loud voice: "Dear Lord, we beseech upon thee to look down upon our humble family and bless this meal. And bless our family, and guide us in the path that thou hast laid before us. We thank thee oh Lord that thou hast brought our son Travis safely back to us and we ask a special blessing for him and may we be in awe of thy greatness and serve thee till the end of our days. Amen."

Ethan had never heard praying like that before. For some reason, it made him ill at ease. The supper was a lot plainer and less tasty than what Ethan's mother would cook, but it was still a good meal of roast beef, boiled potatoes, carrots and dry bread with butter. Everyone came to life and dug in.

"So what have you been doing with yourself lately son?" Mr. Cain asked.

"Ranch work mostly and a few cattle drives."

"He was just on a cattle drive to Wyoming and that's how he became friends with Ethan," Mrs. Cain offered.

"Wyoming, you say. Up to Cheyenne?"

"Yep that's it."

"So I trust you're savin' up your money for the future?"

"Well, I don't know how much I've saved but I definitely have plans for my future. In fact I have some news to tell you about all that." Travis set down his fork, briefly made eye contact with Ethan, then looked at his father. "Ethan and I are going into business together."

Mrs. Cain looked up and a smile crossed her lips.

Mr. Cain didn't bat an eye. "That so. What kind of business?"

"We're going to go into the horse breeding business. We've bought a place in Denver and we're going to find a nice spread to build a horse ranch."

"Oh, that sounds just fine!" Mrs. Cain said. "A horse ranch in Colorado! That's dandy news, Travis. I'm so glad you're gonna settle down somewhere."

"Sounds like a good plan," Mr. Cain said. "Horses are in high demand, especially purebreds."

Ethan was astonished. Travis's parents couldn't be happier to see him go. But it wasn't like they saw that much of him anyhow.

"Of course it's gonna take a lot of money to build a ranch and buy up some breeding stock," Mr. Cain continued.

"We intend to get jobs working in Denver to raise the money."

Mr. Cain nodded his approval.

Once supper was finished, Mrs. Cain served dessert. It was just as plain as the supper had been: canned peaches with fresh cream, and after dessert, everyone spread out a little. Mr. and Mrs. Cain sat in each of the parlor chairs, Travis and Ethan sat on two of the kitchen chairs and the two younger girls played jacks on the kitchen floor. Eva sat at the dining table doing her homework, but she constantly looked up and into the parlor every time Travis had anything to say.

"So how's business at the shop?" Travis asked.

Mr. Cain nodded, stuffing his pipe. "Business is fine. Just fine."

He put Ethan ill at ease. Maybe it was just the terrible things Travis had told him about his father, or else he was sensing something more. Mr. Cain was courteous and polite, but there was something behind his eyes that was like cold steel.

"Are you having second thoughts about giving up the family business?" Mr. Cain said. "I'd still be willing to have you come back and learn the trade so you could take over someday."

Travis didn't have to answer.

"Now Ben," Mrs. Cain said, "you know how Travis feels about that. He's already got his plans in Colorado."

Eyes focused on Travis, he lit the pipe and waved the match in the air to extinguish it. "I know, I know. I just wanted him to know he was welcome to come back if he ever changed his mind. I guess I'm just gonna have to count on Eva. Give her a few more years to grow up, then I'm sure she'll get married and then I'll have a son-in-law to take over for me."

"Speaking of marriage," Mrs. Cain said. Things were already

turning sour. "Travis, did you know that Stephen Foster got married this past spring?"

"What? He did?" Travis seemed startled. "Who did he marry?"

"That young girl Emily Sanders. She's not yet eighteen."

"I'll be darned. I didn't even know he was courting anyone."

Travis's reaction made Ethan wonder just who this Stephen was. Perhaps a close friend? He wondered if Travis had desired Stephen.

"I wish I had have known," Travis said.

"Well, they were barely just engaged when they got married," Mrs. Cain explained. "It wouldn't have done no good to write you to come, because by the time the letter had got to you, wherever you were out there, the wedding would have been said and done."

"Well, I'm just gonna have to go and visit Stephen and his new bride before I leave."

"I was just thinking," Mrs. Cain said, "that the girls can all sleep on the floor in the front room and each of you boys can take one of the bedrooms."

"That won't be necessary, Mother. The girls don't have to give up their rooms. Ethan and I are going to rent rooms at the hotel."

"Travis, you don't have to do that. The girls won't mind at all. It will be fun for them."

"No thanks. We'll be fine at the hotel."

The rest of the evening was spent in pleasant conversation, for Mrs. Cain was a gracious host and Travis stayed busy with Jane and Katie. He pretended to be different animals and the girls would try and guess which. Eva finally abandoned the pretense of doing her homework and joined in with the guessing. They were all having such a good time that before they knew it, the mantle clock chimed ten o'clock. So Travis and Ethan excused themselves with the promise that they would spend as much time as possible with the family before leaving for Denver.

The moon was just a sliver that night as they drove the wagon into town. It was so dark Travis had to drive Cleo at a crawl to keep her from running them off the road. Once they had left the house behind, Ethan touched Travis's wrist.

"Who's Stephen?"

"He was a very good friend of mine." Travis didn't offer any more information but Ethan sensed he was holding something back.

"Did you have desires for him?"

"What?" Travis laughed. "Well, I never really thought about it. He was just my friend. It was long before I knew about myself. But now that you mention it, he was a mighty nice looking fellow and I suppose deep down, I might have had some desires that I wasn't ready to face."

They rode along in silence. Ethan was troubled.

"That was years ago, Ethan," Travis said. "Now he's got a bride and I've got you. He'll never be anything more to me than a good friend." Travis reached over, put his arm around Ethan's shoulders and gave him a one-armed squeeze. "Now let's get to that hotel and I'll show you just how much I love you."

*   *   *

It was Tuesday night. A tall dark figure lurked in the shadows between the buildings across the street from the Italian restaurant. As Travis and Ethan emerged from the restaurant having finished their meal, the figure receded into the shadows and watched. As Travis and Ethan walked along the plank sidewalk, the figure tracked them from across the street, staying in the shadows and in doorways.

They arrived at the hotel some five blocks away. The figure watched them enter, and then he waited. About three minutes later a kerosene lamp lit up the upstairs window. The figure watched as the silhouette of a man came up to the window. The silhouette of a second man joined the first, embracing him from behind. The first silhouette drew the shade and the window was blacked out. The watcher disappeared into the night.

*   *   *

Ethan slept in on Wednesday morning. It was ten-thirty by the time he had gotten himself up and dressed, and Travis had been up and out of the hotel for hours. Ethan finished combing his hair, thinking about the big breakfast he was going to have at the restaurant across the street, when he heard steps pounding in

165

the hall. The door flung open and Travis barged into the room. He had bruises on his face, a black eye, and a cut on his cheek. Blood smeared down the side of his face. Ethan froze in his steps, his mind a whirl of terror as he tried to grasp at a single thought.

"Travis, holy shit..."

Travis went straight to the mirror, turning his head side to side, examining his injuries. "My father. He just beat the tar out of me."

Ethan crowded him around the mirror, reaching up to the cuts. "But why?"

Travis pushed Ethan's hands away. "I don't know how, but he knows about us."

Ethan met Travis's eyes. He wanted to look away, but couldn't.

"Ethan? Did you tell anybody?"

Ethan didn't answer.

"Ethan! Who did you tell?"

"Just Miss Peet." Ethan sat down on the bed. "But I swore her to secrecy. She wouldn't..."

"Dammit Ethan, I warned you never to tell anybody, ever! You can't trust anybody, not even your closest friends."

Travis was really mad. The words stung Ethan as sure as if he had used a whip. Tears welled up in his eyes. He'd ruined their lives.

Travis waved his hand at Ethan. "Don't cry. I'll figure something out." He went to the washbasin, took a washcloth and began cleaning up his cut. Ethan sat on the bed and watched while he gently washed off the dried blood and attached cloth strips over the cuts. He hated Miss Peet. Why had he let her needle him into telling her? She'd made Travis stop loving him, and she got the last evil laugh.

Cleaned and bandaged, Travis looked better.

"Here's what we've got to do," he said. "We have to leave immediately. Tonight. And we'll go someplace where nobody knows us and we can start fresh, and we'll never see our families again. That's the only way out of this mess."

Ethan was unable to speak so he nodded. Travis continued to

think for a while as he formulated a plan. He absentmindedly began to fold his clothes and stuff them into his bag.

"The wagon and Cleo are still in my parents' barn. We'll have to go back there to get them. But first I've got to take care of a few things. So here's what I need you to do. Just stay here in the hotel all day and don't show your face to anybody. And then go to my parents' barn at nine o'clock tonight. I'll meet you there and we can sneak out with Cleo and the wagon. And don't let anybody see you. All right?"

"I'm really sorry Travis. I can't believe I was so stupid. I'm really scared."

He sat there on the bed feeling so pathetic with his nose running and eyes red from crying, so that Travis softened. He squatted down in front of him, looking into his eyes with love. "Hey, everything's going to be okay. We'll survive this. Don't worry."

Chapter Four

A faint half-moon faintly illuminated the Cain homestead, and kerosene lamps lit up all the windows of the house. Ethan very quietly opened up the barn door and went inside. Someone had left the lamp burning. Cleo was in one of the stalls and whinnied softly, and the wagon was packed with Ethan's and Travis's belongings, ready to go. Travis had not yet arrived. He crossed the barn floor to go over and see Cleo.

"You dirty scum." The voice came from behind him.

Looming in the doorway, brandishing an axe, was Mr. Cain. His eyes burned with fiery rage; his voice was raspy and guttural. He bore scarce resemblance of the man Ethan met five nights ago.

"You stinking, filthy pervert! You turned my boy into a goddamn degenerate. And for that you're gonna answer to the Lord." He grabbed the axe with both hands, raised it over his head and lunged at Ethan from twenty feet away.

Ethan stumbled backwards, until he hit the barn wall. Mr. Cain stood over him, the axe descended slowly, and Ethan reacted on instinct. He dropped to his belly and a loud thud shook the barn wall. The axe blade had sunk three inches into the plank where his chest had been. As Mr. Cain struggled to wrest it loose, Ethan crawled away. He crawled along the barn wall until he came to the stall partition and got to his feet. For a moment, his escape to the barn door was clear, but before he could start running, Mr. Cain was in front of him with the axe. Ethan's hand found a flat-bladed manure shovel. He seized it and held it with both hands like a bat. Mr. Cain came at him again, this time swinging the axe at shoulder-height. As the axe came around, Ethan swung the shovel with the strength of panic. The blade clanged against the axe and the axe tore free, and sailed end over end all the way across the barn.

Mr. Cain's knees buckled and he fell to the floor. A large gash lay open on his face; the edge of the shovel blade had caught him square in the temple. His eyes were half-open and glazed over.

Ethan stood holding the shovel, trembling. Then he dropped the weapon on the floor and knelt down over Mr. Cain. He put his hand on his chest. No movement. He really was dead.

Somebody screamed. In the doorway stood Mrs. Cain with her hands cupped over her mouth. Ethan stood up and slowly backed away from the body until he butted up against the barn wall. His knees gave way and his back slid down the boards until he sat on the floor. He covered his face with his hands and just stayed in that position with his elbows on his knees.

Eva, Jane, and Katie came from the house at the sound of their mother's scream. They saw their father lying on the barn floor with blood all over his face, and they too began to cry and scream.

"Girls, back into the house now!" Mrs. Cain was shaking off her shock. "Eva, take your sisters back into the house, and stay there!"

Even though Eva was in hysterics, she managed to obey. She took her sisters' hands and led them away from the barn.

Mrs. Cain didn't enter the barn but just paced back and forth in the doorway, her face growing paler as she slowly sank deeper into shock. Her eyes were vacant, but she kept glancing back at Mr. Cain's body, not knowing what to do. A man and a woman arrived in the doorway. They were neighbors that had heard the commotion and came to see what was happening. They looked into the barn.

"Oh my God," the man said. "I'll go for the sheriff right

away." A few minutes later his horse's hooves beat against the road.

"What's going on?"

"Oh Travis!" cried Mrs. Cain. "Your father!" She began to sob, caving in against Travis's shoulder. Travis held her, eyes searching the barn. He saw his father's body, he saw the shovel, and he saw Ethan sitting up against the wall with his face buried. Travis knew what had happened. He beckoned the neighbor lady and he gently transferred his sobbing mother to her shoulder.

"My husband went to go get the sheriff," she said to him.

Travis ignored the comment and went to Ethan.

"Tell me what happened."

Ethan looked up, still trembling. "He was going to kill me, Travis. He had an axe and he was going to kill me with it. I didn't mean to do it. It was an accident. But he was going to kill me."

"I know. I trust you. When the sheriff gets here, tell him exactly what happened. Anyone can see it was self-defense."

"I didn't mean to do it. He *really* was going to kill me."

"It'll be all right."

About fifteen minutes later, horses galloped up to the barn. Two men dismounted. One was a tall thin man with leathery skin, long grizzled hair and a handlebar mustache. The other was heavy-set and round-faced.

"Mrs. Cain?" the thin man asked looking at the two women waiting to see which would respond.

"Yes."

"Tell me what happened here."

As she talked he surveyed the barn with his eyes.

"My husband came... outside. He didn't... tell me why." Her voice kept breaking, and she tried to compose herself. "I heard some... loud noises. Like banging. So I came out to see what it was. When I got out here, I saw him... over my husband's body." She pointed at Ethan who was still sitting against the wall but was no longer hiding his face.

"Do you know this man?" the Sheriff asked.

"Yes. He's a friend of my son Travis." She pointed at Travis.

"And then what happened?"

"I screamed. The neighbors came. And that's all."

"And where was your son?"

"He came just before you did."

"Uh-huh. So nobody else was here when you came out?"

"No."

The sheriff then went over to Ethan.

"Get up on your feet, boy."

Ethan rose.

"You wanna tell me what happened?"

"Mr. Cain was trying to kill me, I had to defend myself."

"What were you doing here, in the barn?"

"I came to meet Travis."

"Why?"

Travis then spoke up. "We were meeting to make plans to get on the road. We were planning to leave town."

The sheriff looked at Travis for a long time, as if waiting for a better answer. Ethan nodded in agreement.

"Okay, so you came to the barn, then what exactly happened?"

"Mr. Cain came into the barn. He had an axe and he said he was going to kill me. He came at me with the axe, but he missed. So I went for the shovel and he came at me again and I swung the shovel at him to get the axe away from him, but the shovel must have hit him in the head. It was an accident. I didn't mean to kill him."

"He acted in self defense," Travis interjected.

"And how would you know that" the sheriff asked, "if you weren't here?"

"No I wasn't here. I didn't come until just a few minutes ago."

"You wanna tell me what happened to your face?"

"I was in a fight this morning."

"With who?"

"With him." Travis pointed to the body.

"Okay." He turned back to Ethan. "Your name is Ethan, you say? What's your full name?"

"Ethan Keller."

"And where are you from?"

Ethan told him the name of the town he lived in.

"Mr. Keller, I'm afraid we're going to have to take you in until we can get this all sorted out. Take him on in, Amos."

Travis was stone-faced as Deputy Amos handcuffed Ethan and patted down his entire body, searching for weapons. He led Ethan outside and mounted his horse.

"You're gonna walk to the jailhouse. And don't even *think* of doin' anything funny. I'll shoot you dead before you can even get twenty steps away."

It was about a thirty minute walk to the sheriff's office and jailhouse. Ethan walked silently in the moonlight while the deputy, his rifle in the crook of his arm, rode his horse alongside. Sleeping farmhouses and barns passed by on both sides of the deserted road, indifferent to their passage. When they arrived, the deputy removed his handcuffs and confiscated the only things he had in his pockets – his coin pouch, a comb, a neckerchief, and a ring with two tiny keys to his trunk. The sheriff's office consisted of a room with two desks, a cot and a gun rack. A door led to another room containing four cells. The deputy locked Ethan in the farthest one, furnished with a cot, a ratty-looking blanket and bowl in the corner for urine.

Ethan sat down on the cot. "What's going to happen to me?"

Deputy Amos appeared to be irritated by the question.

"That's for the sheriff to decide. You shut up and wait." He went back into the office, leaving the door open and took a Winchester '73 rifle out of the rack. Ethan could no longer see him as he sat at the desk, but he could hear him disassemble the gun and begin brushing out the chambers. Soon the smell of gun oil penetrated the tang of the urine bowl.

Around ten-thirty the deputy came back into the cell block and turned out the kerosene lamp. Ethan sat on the bed in complete darkness, his mind racing. In *A Tale of Two Cities*, Charles, an innocent man, had been jailed by the revolutionaries for the crimes of his family. In the book Charles was sentenced to the guillotine. Of course, Charles was saved when his look-alike died in his place. But that was just a story. Ethan had no double. He fretted into the wee hours of the morning until finally, exhausted from stress, he laid back and fell into a deep sleep.

Chapter Five

Deputy Amos brought Ethan some breakfast the next morning, finding him sitting on the bed with his blanket neatly folded beside him. The meal consisted of cold oatmeal and two stale pieces of bread. Ethan was so hungry he ate it, thinking of the last breakfast his mother had prepared him of bacon, and a tasty omelet. Now that it was daylight, he could see his surroundings more clearly. The back wall was made of brick and there was one barred window near the ceiling, just out of reach. The floor was wooden. Ethan wondered why a convict couldn't just break through the floor and dig his way out. Then he noticed that the bars continued on through little holes in the floorboards. Except for the brick wall, he was basically in a cage. The floor was covered with dust and dirt, the cot was stained and the blanket smelled like old cheese. The urine bowl was more potent today from his own addition an hour ago. He finished his oatmeal and left the bowl on the floor by the cell door. There was nothing to do but wait and think.

The sounds from outside gave him some idea of the time. There had been a bustle of traffic in the morning with wagons going by, and people opening up their businesses, but all was quiet now. So much time had gone by he knew it must be well past noon, but then he heard a drunk stumble by and ask someone if they could spare a penny or two so he could buy some breakfast.

Somewhere around eleven o'clock the sheriff came to see him.

"Mr. Keller." The sheriff stood three feet away from the bars. Ethan stood up.

"You are formally being charged with the murder of Benjamin Cain. The charge is murder in the first degree and your trial is set for a week from today. Do you have a lawyer?"

Ethan felt the oatmeal in his stomach threatening to come back up. "No."

"If you're unable to get a lawyer, we will appoint one to defend you. He tipped his hat and left.

Ethan stood for a second staring at the closed door. How the hell could they do this? He picked up the urine bowl, screamed at the top of his lungs and hurled it against the bars, splattering the stinking piss all over the floor inside and outside the bars. The bowl clattered to the floor and he grabbed the bars with both hands and shook as hard as he could, barely making them rattle. "God damn it, it's not fair! Let me out of here!"

*   *   *

That afternoon Travis came into the sheriff's office. Deputy Amos was leaning back in his chair with his feet up on the desk.

"I'd like to see the prisoner."

"What for?"

"I have a right."

"You know that this guy murdered your father, don't you?"

Travis didn't answer.

"You're not going to rough him up are you?"

"No, I just want to talk to him."

"I'm gonna have to search you."

Travis lifted his arms and spread his legs compliantly. After patting down his sides and up his inseams, and checking in the tops of his boots, Amos was satisfied and took him into the room with the cells. Ethan jumped up at the sight of Travis.

"Travis! They've charged me with murder –"

"I know."

Deputy Amos stood in the doorway watching.

"May we have some privacy?" Travis asked. The deputy

scowled, then turned and left, closing the door behind him.

"They don't believe me Travis. They're charging me with first degree murder!"

"I know, I know. It's going to be okay, Ethan. They can't possibly find you guilty at the trial." Travis's voice was distant, somehow less forceful than normal. He fumbled with the brim of his hat. "I've sent for your family. They should be here sometime tonight. Ethan, I want you to try not to worry. We'll get you out and then we will go away together just like we planned. Be strong for me okay?"

Ethan nodded.

"And one other thing. They're probably not going to let me see you again. But even though you may not see me, just know that I'm still here for you, okay?"

"Okay."

Travis quickly kissed Ethan through the bars and then went out the door. Ethan was again left in silence. But that one little kiss, and the message Travis had given him, made all the difference. It gave him hope. He lay back down on the bed and waited some more, still worried, but patient.

*   *   *

When the door opened again, Ethan knew by the deep snores of the drunks outside his window that it was very late at night. He sat up on his cot. He hadn't yet fallen asleep. Deputy Amos escorted another visitor into the room – Willie. Amos pointed at the last cell and stepped back out, leaving them alone. Willie came over to face Ethan, who was already standing behind the bars watching him. Willie took a few moments to look over the whole room. The flickering of the lamp cast shadows of the bars all over the walls. Ethan was glad to see another familiar face. They were both aware of the irony of the situation of which side of the bars each of them was on.

"Well, well, little brother. You're in a fix now aren't you?"

"Where's Ma?"

"She didn't come, Ethan. As soon as she heard what happened, she was so upset she made herself sick. She had to go straight to bed."

"She's not coming at all then?"

"You know she can't deal with it, Ethan. She's weak."

Ethan swallowed hard. "I'm innocent you know. It was self-defense."

"Of course I know that. You don't think I know what my little brother's capable of? You wouldn't hurt a fly. I know you musta been protecting yourself."

"Thanks, Willie."

"Know what I've been doing since I got here? I hired you a lawyer. I met up with that Travis guy and he helped me find you the best lawyer in all of San Antone. He's expensive, but he'll see that you don't get hanged."

Ethan was amazed. "But how did you pay for him? Where'd you get the money?"

"Just don't you concern yourself about that."

Great. His defense was going to be paid for with money from stolen cows.

"Thanks, Willie."

"You know I always look out for my little brother. Your lawyer's name is Mr. Emerson. I'll bring him to see you tomorrow morning. So I'll see you then." Willie tipped his hat and danced a few little steps of a jig, pointed at Ethan with his forefinger, thumb cocked, winked and clicked his tongue before he stepped out the door.

*   *   *

Deputy Amos let Willie and Mr. Emerson in the jail cell, dragged in two chairs for them, and locked them all in together. Mr. Emerson was a thin man, a little shorter than Ethan, and about thirty-five years old. His black hair was parted in the middle and oiled. Dressed in a precisely tailored brown suit and bowtie, he wore round spectacles and had a pencil-line mustache. Using his briefcase on his lap for a writing surface, Mr. Emerson set out to gain the full story in a quiet non-threatening manner.

"All right, Mr. Keller. First I need to get a little background so I can see the entire picture. How did you know Mr. Benjamin Cain?"

"I'm a good friend of his son Travis."

"And you were here in town visiting Travis?"

"Yes."

"And before that night, how did you and Mr. Cain get along?"

"Which Mr. Cain do you mean?"

"Mr. Benjamin Cain."

"Okay I guess. He treated me politely."

"Now I need you to describe the events of last Wednesday night. He looked at Ethan over the top of his spectacles. "Don't leave anything out."

Ethan told the edited story as he remembered it. He didn't make reference to the true nature of his relationship with Travis and he omitted the part where Mr. Cain had called him a pervert and had accused him of turning Travis into a degenerate.

"So do you have any idea why Mr. Cain turned on you this way? Why did he want to kill you?"

Ethan remembered Travis's urgent warning to trust no one, and a little too late. "I have no idea."

"Now Mr. Keller, I can't be of any service to you unless you are completely honest and tell me everything. There has to be a reason why Mr. Cain wanted to kill you."

Ethan shook his head.

"It's okay to tell him, little brother. You can trust him," Willie said.

"That's right. It's called attorney-client privilege and by law I can't reveal anything you tell me without your consent."

Ethan hesitated. Should he tell them? Travis's warnings had not made allowances for any special circumstances. Maybe he could deal in half-truths.

"Mr. Cain *may* have thought that Travis and I were sodomites."

Ethan expected Willie to recoil, but he didn't. He was completely unfazed. Apparently everyone already knew about it.

"A-ha!" Mr. Emerson exclaimed. "Now we're getting somewhere. Mr. Cain, having heard rumors about you and his son, now had a motive to kill you – to protect his son."

Ethan told him the actual words Mr. Cain had used before trying to kill him.

"But of course the accusations against you and Travis Cain are entirely false." Mr. Emerson said in a manner that sounded much more like a statement than a question.

"Of course."

"The last thing I'm going to need is a character witness. Who do you know that would testify on your behalf? A friend or someone you worked closely with? Someone who knows you quite well and likes you?"

"How about Travis?"

"Well, if the prosecution introduces the sodomy angle, and they most probably will, Mr. Cain's testimony will be worthless. Anyone else?"

"I'll testify for him." Willie said.

"If need be I'll put you on the stand, but generally testimony from close family members doesn't hold much weight. The jury knows that family sticks together and will go so far as to commit perjury to protect one another. I still need another name."

"How about Miss Peet?" Ethan said.

"Who is Miss Peet?"

"She's the schoolmarm. She was my teacher, and a real good friend."

"Please tell me you were a good student."

"I was. She said I was her best pupil."

He jabbed his pencil in the air, his pencil-line mustache straightening out on his lip as he smiled. "That's perfect! Exactly the kind of witness I was looking for – someone who observed you and can vouch that you had a strong moral character." He began to pack up his pencil and notes. "I trust I have everything I need for now. I should be in contact with you again before the trial."

*   *   *

The next four days were miserable again. He had no visitors, or at least none he was allowed to see, and he began to regret he hadn't asked Willie for a book. Meals were a few scraps of dry meat with beans and stale bread served cold and the only times he was let out of his cell was when he had to release his bowels. And then he would be handcuffed and escorted at gunpoint by Deputy Amos who would stand guard at the outhouse. He had no activities to occupy his time and the window in his cell was so high up, all he could see was sky. Occasionally there would be some commotion outside and he would strain to hear what was going on, but it was usually just one or the other of the two drunks who lived outside, whom he could tell apart by their snores. He almost wished they would arrest another prisoner so he would have someone to talk to. He wasn't even able to keep track of the passage of the time by the meals, as Amos served them irregularly just to be cruel.

Finally, on Tuesday afternoon, he got another visit from his lawyer and Willie. They were again locked into the cell with him, and Willie tried to cheer him up by patting him on the back and by reassuring him that everything was going to work out and he would be out in less than a week. He also pulled a book out of his back pocket and handed it to him. It was folded in half and had no doubt just been purchased from the store. *The Adventures of Buffalo Bill Cody.* A dime novel. Ethan thought of Dolores.

"Tell him, Mr. Emerson," Willie said, "Tell him he'll be out in no time."

Mr. Emerson had no interest in Ethan's state of mind; he was simply there to conduct business. He pulled a pad and an expensive looking fountain pen out of his briefcase and adjusted his spectacles on his nose.

"Unfortunately we won't be able to use Miss Peet as a character witness," Mr. Emerson said.

"What? Why not?" Ethan asked.

"Well, it turns out she's already been summoned to testify for the prosecution. She's going to testify against you."

"I have half a mind to go and teach that Miss Peet a thing or two," Willie snarled.

"No, no. None of that. You'll only make things worse. We don't even know what she's going to say yet. Let's just concentrate on what we need to do next. We need to find another character witness, Mr. Keller. Do you have any suggestions?"

Ethan's head was reeling from the shock. He really didn't have any close friends. He was surprised to realize that he never trusted anyone enough to get close to them, not before Travis.

"How about jobs? Surely you've had a boss that was pleased with you, Mr. Keller."

Ethan began to wonder if Mr. Emerson was merely going

through formalities. Had he already collected all the relevant facts from Willie?

"Oh yes. There's Mr. Simpson. He's the owner of the general store. I worked for him for nearly a year."

"And he was pleased with your work?" Mr. Emerson scribbled notes on the pad, not having looked up even once.

"As far as I know. Um… Mr. Emerson?"

"Yes?"

"How are things looking? I mean, what are our chances of winning?"

"Things are looking okay. I think we have a good chance to win." He met Ethan's eye briefly then capped his fountain pen.

Chapter Six

The morning of the trial, the sun shone brightly in the jail cell window. Ethan was not heartened by it. Mr. Emerson stopped by the jailhouse and dropped off some new clothes and a list of instructions with an admonition to the deputy that they be followed to the letter.

Deputy Amos entered the room and unlocked his cell.

"Well don't just sit there like a jackass," the deputy said. "Get up. We got places to go." He slapped the handcuffs on Ethan and led him out of the cell room into the sheriff's office. He made sure Ethan was watching as he hoisted the revolver in his holster and re-situated it under his belly. He picked up the stack of clothes on the desk and pushed Ethan out the door, walking behind him on the wooden plank sidewalk. Ethan had no sense of where they were going in town that was still unfamiliar, and kept turning around to look at the deputy who in turn kept shoving him in the back to keep him moving. After walking a few blocks, the deputy stopped him in front of a bathhouse.

"In here."

Inside behind the counter, a short, rotund, white-haired lady raised her eyebrows at the sight of the prisoner, but asked no questions.

"A bath for the prisoner," Deputy Amos said.

"Yes sir, right this way." She led them to a back room and began warming up the bathtub by pouring buckets of hot water into the already half-full tub. Once she was finished she exited the room and closed the door.

Ethan looked at the deputy.

"What are you waitin' for?" the deputy barked. "Strip down and get in the bathtub!"

"Aren't you going to give me some privacy?"

"Hell, no!" He unlocked the handcuffs and Ethan undressed as quickly as he could, keeping his back to the deputy, and got into the bathtub. He quickly washed himself, got out of the bath and started to put on the clothes.

"No, these," said the deputy. They were brand new clothes and much nicer than any he'd ever worn: a tan shirt, dark brown trousers and coat, a tie, and new shoes. They fit rather well, though not perfect, and the workmanship was as good as if his mother had sewn them.

Their next stop was the barbershop. For this, Ethan remained handcuffed. The deputy sat in a chair and waited while the barber shaved Ethan's few whiskers and gave him a haircut, combed his hair and patted his jaw and neck with a splash of eau de toilette.

As they were walking down the sidewalk, Ethan caught a glimpse of his reflection in a store window. His mother would have said he looked handsome – all grown up.

Ethan looked back at the deputy. "Thank you for this."

Amos frowned with his mouth half open, then sneered. "Don't be a jackass."

Ethan saw by the deputy's pocket watch that it was about noon. The deputy escorted him through the courthouse's plain large door, only a few blocks from the sheriff's office. It was a simple building with a single courtroom, a vestibule in the front and judge's chambers in the back. The courtroom held the bench, the witness chair, a jury box, tables for the prosecution and defense, and four short rows of seats for spectators. The bench sat atop a high dais and the witness chair and jury box on two lower ones. The pine trim around the bench and jury box was sanded and polished.

Ethan, still in handcuffs, took his seat next to Mr. Emerson at the defense table. People slowly began filing into the courtroom. Every time someone entered, Ethan turned around to see if it was anyone he knew. Once he turned around to see Travis and Mrs. Cain take their seats in the front row. They were dressed in black and Mrs. Cain wore a veil over her face. Travis briefly made eye contact with him but for both their sakes showed no sense of recognition. A little while later Willie entered. He sat down in the front row a few seats away from the Cains and nodded at Ethan. By the time court was ready to commence, only half the spectator seats had been filled. A newspaper reporter with a pad and pencil sat on the end seat of the front row. The rest of the spectators were mostly curious citizens who sought the entertainment of seeing a murderer sentenced to hang.

A young, well-dressed short man with a neatly trimmed beard entered the courtroom carrying a briefcase. His gaze darted around the room as he plopped the briefcase down on the prosecution's table and sat down behind it. He opened the briefcase and began rifling through the papers; he was either unprepared or nervous. Ethan wondered how many cases he had tried; he guessed not many. His lawyer was sedate by comparison. Mr. Emerson showed no signs of stress at all as he sat staring straight ahead quietly tapping his pencil. An assistant carried in a five-foot long object wrapped in burlap and placed it under the prosecutor's table. Ethan guessed it was the murder weapon. The prosecutor finally got all his papers in order and began reading them over. Twenty minutes passed by the clock on the wall behind the jury box. A tall, slim, older man in uniform, mostly bald with a few strands of gray hair combed over, entered from the back of the room and stood against the wall opposite the jury box. He crossed his arms and waited. The judge finally emerged from his chambers. He was a large man, well over six feet tall with iron-gray hair and baggy skin under his cheeks and cool gray eyes. Ethan looked into his face, searching for a trace of kindness in those eyes. The judge didn't make eye contact with him and showed no expression at all, kind or otherwise.

"All rise for the honorable Judge Jones," said the bailiff.

"Court is now in session," Judge Jones said banging his gavel on the desk. "Please bring in the jury."

The door opened from the vestibule and the bailiff led the jurors to the box. He then crossed the room and took his place next to the deputy.

The jury consisted of twelve men that had been informally selected from the townsfolk. Some were businessmen dressed in suits and some were farmers in coveralls. They took their seats and many of them looked Ethan over with contempt. Not a word had been spoken against him, yet he felt that many of them already judged him guilty. The bailiff swore in the jury, and had them sit.

"We are ready for your opening statements, Mr. Dreyer," the judge said to the prosecutor. Mr. Dreyer rose, placed himself in front of the jury box and addressed the jury. Before he even spoke the first word, he was interrupted by the eldest member of the jury, a crotchety, bent-over farmer with sun-wrinkled skin and a few wisps of white hair on his bald head.

"Judge, ain't you got no spittoon in this here court? I'd sure hate to dirty up this nice clean floor, but where's a man to spit?"

The judge gave a heavy sigh. "Deputy, see if you can find this juror something to accommodate his vice."

Deputy Amos left the courtroom. The Judge motioned for Mr. Dreyer to continue. Mr. Dreyer cleared his throat. He spoke in a forceful, preacher's voice, but never took his eyes off the paper he held in his hand.

"Kind citizens of San Antonio, you have all been selected to try this man, Mr. Ethan Keller, on the charge of murder in the first degree of one Mr. Benjamin Cain. It is my intention to prove to you that he is guilty of this crime. Through testimony and physical evidence, I will prove to you that he had motive and means to commit the crime. After weighing all the testimony and evidence, it is my opinion that you will have no other choice but to convict. Thank you." Mr. Dreyer walked back to his table and sat down. Beads of sweat had formed on his forehead.

"Mr. Emerson, please proceed with your opening statements."

Mr. Emerson crossed the room to address the jurors just as Mr. Dreyer had, but he was more at ease. He leaned on the banister and made direct eye contact with each of the jurors as he spoke, his words having been committed to memory.

"Fellow citizens, while it is true that my client, Mr. Ethan Keller, did kill the alleged victim, Mr. Benjamin Cain, I will prove to you that this was not in fact murder, but self-defense. Mr. Keller is an upstanding citizen who has never been in trouble with the law. I will provide witnesses to his character and it is my intent to prove that all of the prosecution's evidence is erroneous. After you have heard all the testimony and evidence you will find my client not guilty."

As Mr. Emerson walked confidently back to his seat, at least two of the jurors made an audible "Humph."

"Are you ready to call your first witness, Mr. Dreyer?" asked the judge.

"I am, Your Honor. I would like to call to the stand Sheriff Roy Cochrane."

The sheriff took the stand and was sworn in by the bailiff.

"Sheriff Cochrane, could you please tell us what you were able to ascertain from the crime scene when you arrived?"

The Sheriff was completely at ease on the stand. He was accustomed to testifying in court trials, and took his time to carefully answer the question.

"Well, when I got there, I saw Mr. Cain layin' on his side in the middle of the barn floor with his face all cut up and a shovel layin' beside him. The defendant was sittin' against the back wall of the barn and Mrs. Cain was standing with a neighbor woman and she was upset. Mr. Travis Cain, the victim's son, was off by himself walkin' around the barn. So I questioned Mrs. Cain first. She said that her husband had come out of the house and after a while she heard some banging noises and came out to see what was happening, and she saw Mr. Keller crouched down over her husband and the shovel layin' beside him. Then she screamed and the neighbors came. Next I questioned Mr. Keller. He said that Mr. Cain was tryin' to kill *him*. He said Mr. Cain came at him with an axe and he used the shovel to get the axe away from him and *accidentally* hit Mr. Cain in the head."

"Did you search the barn, Sheriff?"

"Yes I did."

"And did you find an axe?"

"No. There was no axe anywhere in that barn." The Sheriff looked Ethan directly in the eye as he made this accusation.

Ethan's jaw dropped. How could there be no axe?

"Please continue, Sheriff."

"Well, I asked Mr. Keller what he was doin' in the barn and he said he come to meet up with Travis Cain so they could leave town together. I then questioned Travis and he said he had only arrived just before me and found everything exactly as it was when I got there. I also noticed he had bruises and a black eye so I asked him about it and he said he had been in a fight with his father, Mr. Cain, that morning. Well I thought this all seemed rather suspicious so I had my deputy take Mr. Keller in while I searched the barn and brought in the body."

"Thank you, Sheriff. Oh, one more thing." Mr. Dreyer pulled the shovel out from under the table and unwrapped it. "Is this the shovel you found lying next to the victim's body?" He held the object, horizontally in front of the sheriff. Ethan stared at the shovel. It looked no different than any other barnyard shovel, but the sight of it made his throat close up.

"Yes it is."

"Thank you, Sheriff Cochrane. That is all." He placed the shovel on a table in full view. Its hard metal was dull and scored, wood handle soiled. "Mr. Emerson, you may cross-examine if you wish."

"Sheriff Cochrane," Mr. Emerson began forcefully, and rose from his seat but stayed behind the desk. "In your opinion, after a man has committed a murder with intent, does he generally stick around and wait to be taken in or does he flee the scene?"

"Well, of course normally he would flee."

"Then, in your opinion, if the defendant had willfully committed this murder, why did he not flee?"

"I don't know. Perhaps he wasn't too smart."

"You've interviewed the defendant. Do you believe he is mentally deficient?"

"Well then maybe it was all part of his plan to kill Mr. Cain and then claim it was self-defense. It's been known to happen that way."

"Answer the question…"

"No, I would not say he's mentally deficient."

"How many murderers have you arrested that didn't flee and claimed they acted in self-defense?"

"Well, none personally. But I've heard of it before."

"Thank you, Sheriff. No more questions." Mr. Emerson sat down and scribbled a few notes.

"The prosecution now calls to the stand Doctor Arthur Hinkley," said Mr. Dreyer, his voice weak and unsure.

*   *   *

Fatigue made Travis's mind wander. As soon as he left Ethan at the jailhouse a week ago, he had gone all over town in search of a lawyer. Even though his mother was distraught and needed him to help her with the funeral preparations, he abandoned her to manage on her own because he'd chosen Ethan over his family long ago. He had no experience in retaining a lawyer and started by asking some of the local businessmen for a recommendation. None had any, but they sent him to other people they knew who might be of help. And those contacts would send him to yet others so that he began to feel he was on a fool's errand. But it finally paid off when a banker was able to give him the name of Roland Emerson, who was believed to be the best defense lawyer in San Antone. The banker said he was young, but he was shrewd and had a good track record for getting acquittals. Of course he was expensive. Travis paid Mr. Emerson a visit in his cluttered, yet roomy office, told him the whole story – for the most part – and asked him to take the case. Mr. Emerson was intrigued and extended his hand. Travis had given him all the money he had left from the cattle drive, though it wasn't near enough to cover his fee. When Willie arrived later that night, Travis was relieved to find that he had brought more than enough money to pay the lawyer, and asked no questions about its source.

Travis lay awake most nights sick with worry and when he did finally drop off his terrible nightmares claimed him. A recurring one had him lost in the woods searching for Ethan. He would chase the sounds of laughing cowboys throughout the woods until he would finally come upon Ethan naked, hogtied and being raped by one of the cowboys from the cattle drive. The rest of the cowboys stood around laughing and waiting their turn. Miss Peet was there with a red-hot branding iron. She took the iron and branded Ethan on the buttocks, looking maliciously at Travis while Ethan screamed in pain. "Look what you've done to this poor boy!" she hissed.

Travis forced his attention back to the trial as the judge was swearing in a gray-haired rotund man wearing spectacles and appearing to be about sixty years old.

Mr. Dreyer dabbed the sweat from his forehead with a handkerchief. "Doctor Hinkley, I believe you examined the body of the victim, Mr. Benjamin Cain?"

"Yes I did."

"And could you tell us, in your medical opinion, what was the cause of death?"

"The cause of death was a direct blow to the head. The weapon hit him in the temple with such force that it caused his brain to hemorrhage. He most likely died within seconds."

"And were you able to identify the murder weapon, Doctor?"

"Yes I was. The shape of the cut on the side of his face was consistent with the edge of the shovel blade that was brought to me."

"And is this the shovel you examined?" Mr. Dreyer held up the shovel.

"Yes it is."

"Thank you, Doctor. That is all."

"You may cross-examine, Mr. Emerson."

"No questions, Your Honor."

"Very well, next witness."

"The prosecution calls to the stand Miss Clara Peet."

Ethan stiffened in his seat. He began to sweat. He felt a churning in his stomach and he struggled not to hyperventilate, fearing of what Miss Peet might tell them. Mr. Hinkley was still making his way out of the courtroom as the sheriff opened the door and summoned Miss Peet. She walked down the aisle with her head held high, looking straight ahead and ignoring Ethan. She was dressed in a magnificent plum dress with pearl buttons and a smart looking hat with a feather to match. Her blonde hair was beautifully pinned up on the back of her neck. She stepped up to the witness chair, faced the spectators, raised her right hand and placed the other one on the Bible.

"Do you swear to tell the truth, the whole truth, and nothing but the truth so help you God?" the bailiff asked.

"I do," she answered with a haughty note in her voice that Ethan had never heard before. She sat down and in her lap she tightly clutched her matching plum-colored purse with both hands.

"Could you state your full name please?" Mr. Dreyer asked.

"Clara Elizabeth Peet."

"Miss Peet, what is your relationship to the defendant?"

"I was his schoolteacher and after that, his friend."

"You had a conversation with the defendant, Mr. Keller, on Friday, September twenty-seventh, did you not?"

"I did."

"And could you please tell the court what he revealed to you in that conversation?"

Ethan's hand went to his stomach, and gently clutched it under the table.

"He told me that he and Travis Cain were in love."

The entire courtroom erupted with a collective gasp of titilation.

Mr. Emerson immediately jumped up. "Your Honor, I object!"

"On what grounds?"

"Relevance, Your Honor. My client is *not* on trial for sodomy. I fail to see how any of this has any relevance to the case."

"I agree. Mr. Dreyer, what is your relevance?"

"Um... it goes to character, Your Honor. If I can prove through testimony that the defendant is indeed a sodomite, it would stand to reason that a person with such degenerate morals would not be above murder."

"That's a bit of a stretch, Mr. Dreyer. Is that all your have?"

"Um...well Your Honor...no. It will establish a motive."

The judge raised his eyebrows. "How so?"

"Your Honor, if I can establish through testimony that the

defendant is a sodomite and that Mr. Travis Cain was the object of his desire, and if the victim had found out about it and were trying to get his son to break off his friendship with the defendant, then the defendant would see the victim as an obstacle and would have motive to get rid of it."

"There are an awful lot of if's in your argument, Mr. Dreyer. Do you have any evidence to show that the victim did indeed have knowledge of the sodomy accusations?"

"Well… there were rumors circulating all over town regarding the nature of the relationship between the defendant and Mr. Travis Cain at the time of the murder. If Your Honor finds it necessary, I could produce witnesses to testify to that."

"Very well, I'll allow it. Objection overruled." He banged his gavel. Mr. Emerson threw up his hands in disbelief and then sat down defeated.

"You may continue questioning the witness, Mr. Dreyer."

"Miss Peet, please continue. You were telling us what the defendant had revealed to you in conversation."

"Yes. Mr. Keller told me that he was in love with Travis Cain and that they were going to move to Wyoming to live together and raise horses."

It was Colorado; not that that would make any difference to the jury. Ethan tried to control his facial expression. He didn't even dare to turn around and look at Travis.

"Did you and the defendant have any other conversation that pertained to his relationship with Mr. Cain?"

"I told him I was not comfortable discussing it with him and he begged me not to tell anyone about it."

Ethan was dismayed at this distortion. It was *she* who had begged *him* for the information.

"Thank you, Miss Peet. No further questions." Miss Peet rose to leave.

"Just a moment, ma'am." the judge said. "We must now give the defense a chance to cross-examine you." She looked startled, but retook her seat. "Your witness, Mr. Emerson."

"Your Honor, may I have a few moments to consult with my client?"

"You may."

Mr. Emerson whispered something to Ethan, and Ethan in turn whispered something back. He stood up and addressed the witness.

"Miss Peet. Did the defendant tell you that he had sodomized Mr. Travis Cain?"

"Why, no."

"Did he tell you that Mr. Cain had sodomized him?"

"No."

"Did he in fact describe any acts at all of a sexual nature that he had practiced with Mr. Cain?"

"Of course not."

"The only thing he did tell you about his relationship with Mr. Cain is that they were in love, is that not the case?"

"Well, yes. But one can conclude from that..."

"One can conclude nothing from that, Miss Peet!" Mr. Emerson interrupted. "Love is an emotion, not an act. And neither our city nor state legislature has yet passed laws against emotions. Now, you say the defendant was your student."

"Yes."

"What was he like in school? Did he get good grades? Was he a good student?"

"Well...he was a satisfactory student. I would say maybe somewhat above average."

"How about his demeanor? Was he well behaved and well liked?"

"His behavior was acceptable in the classroom, I suppose. But I really have no idea about what kind of trouble he got into outside of class."

Any affection or admiration he had for her drained away, and for the first time in his life he felt hatred. She was a sworn enemy to him. But hatred. Is that not what Mr. Cain had felt toward him? If what he felt toward Miss Peet could motivate a person – motivate him – to take her life. The thought repulsed him. He didn't hate her, but she no longer existed in his heart.

"I'm through with this witness, Your Honor."

"You may step down, ma'am," said the judge. Miss Peet slowly got up and found her way out.

"Do you have any more witnesses, Mr. Dreyer?"

"No, Your Honor. The prosecution rests."

"Very well. The defense shall proceed to call its first witness."

* * *

Travis had a sinking feeling in his gut. His armpits were wet and he had to fight to stay calm and not betray his emotions. The jurors now would make assumptions about the sodomy and they would just as soon hang him for it. A look of horror and distaste passed across their faces when Miss Peet let that bull out of the pen. Travis sat gazing at the back of Ethan's neck. He was no more the fifteen feet away. Ethan looked so handsome sitting there. Travis longed to be able to gently stroke that beautiful smooth alabaster skin where his hairline touched the tendons and muscles. He wished he could come up behind him and nuzzle it with his lips. But that provoked another thought – the thought of that lovely neck being stretched out by a rope. One image kept prodding him from a hidden corner of his mind. He constantly pushed it away so he wouldn't have to think about it, but it kept surfacing. It was the image of Ethan standing on the gallows with a noose draped around his throat. He pictured the hangman standing beside him, his head covered with a burlap sack as though the anonymity somehow released him from the guilt of taking a life. Ethan's warm brown eyes gazed lovingly at him as the trap door fell open. His body dropped and the rope cracked his neck bones with a sharp snap. If this were to become a reality, Travis could not go on. He would purchase a gun and kill the hangman, the sheriff and the deputy, grab Ethan and ride away as far as he could go, or a piece of him would die too.

"Your Honor, I would like to call back to the stand, Sheriff Roy Cochrane," Mr. Emerson said.

"Sheriff Cochrane you are still under oath," the judge said to him as he sat back down in the witness chair.

"Sheriff, in light of this new evidence that rumors about my client have been spread around the city, in your opinion, and assuming the victim had knowledge of these rumors, would that not give him motive to attack my client?"

"I suppose it could. If he were the type to be prone to violence."

"And to your knowledge was Mr. Benjamin Cain prone to violence?"

"No. Nothing exceptin' a few bar fights."

"Thank you, Sheriff."

"Mr. Dreyer, do you desire to cross-examine?"

"No, Your Honor."

"You may step down. Next witness, Mr. Emerson."

"I would like to call to the stand Mr. Orville Simpson."

After the swearing in, Mr. Emerson began questioning him amicably.

"Mr. Simpson, how do you know my client, Mr. Keller?"

"He worked for me in my store. He was a stock boy."

"And how long was he employed by you?"

"For about eleven months."

"And in all that time how would you describe his work ethic? By that I mean, was he a good employee for you?"

"Absolutely. He worked real hard and always finished up whatever he had to do. He never missed a day of work, except when he got sick, and he was real friendly-like to the customers. Always helping them out and carrying their merchandise."

"So you would say he had a congenial manner. That is, he never argued or fought with the customers."

"Oh no, never."

"What did you observe about his nature when he wasn't on the job? When you would see him around town, how did he act?"

"Well, he never bothered nobody and he mainly stayed off by himself. Mostly reading them books of his."

"So you never saw him get involved in any mischief or fighting?"

"Ethan? Oh no. Ethan is one of the best behaved lads in the whole town."

"Thank you, Mr. Simpson."

"You may cross-examine now, Mr. Dreyer," the judge said.

"Thank you, Your Honor, but I have no questions for this witness."

"Next witness, Mr. Emerson."

"I call Mr. William Keller to the stand."

Willie strode up to the stand, took the oath and was seated. Ethan was a little surprised that Mr. Emerson decided to have Willie testify, given that Willie's testimony wouldn't carry much weight. He wondered if it was because Miss Peet's testimony had been so damning that he changed his mind. He noticed for the first time that Willie was wearing new clothes and had been freshly barbered too; he looked downright *respectable*.

"Mr. Keller, you are the defendant's older brother?"

"Yessir."

"In your own words, tell us what kind of a man your brother is."

"He's a real good kid. He never hurt nobody and he's real gentle-like. I know he's not capable of doing what you all say. Heck, he does his best to keep *me* outta trouble! And what Miss Peet said about him is totally false. He was the best student she ever had."

"Your Honor," Mr. Dryer objected. "I ask that the witness be instructed not to impugn the integrity of other witnesses and restrict his answers to the questions he is asked."

"Mr. Keller, please do not attack the other witnesses. Just tell us about the defendant," the judge agreed. "The jury will disregard the remark about Miss Peet. Go on, Mr. Keller."

"Well, he *was* a good student and he's real book-smart, too. He reads all the time. He's never gotten into any fights and he's always looking out for me and our ma. I know that when he says he was defending himself, it's true."

"Thank you, Mr. Keller."

"Do you care to cross-examine this one, Mr. Dreyer?"

"Yes, your honor. Mr. Keller, have you ever been in trouble with the law?"

"Well, yeah. A few times, I guess."

"A few times, you say? I checked with the sheriff in your town and would you be surprised to know you've been locked up twenty-two times?"

"I guess but…"

"Tell us what you were locked up for, Mr. Keller."

"Bar fightin', mostly."

"Yes, bar fighting, disturbing the peace, vandalism, theft and assault. No more questions!"

"Your Honor, the defense now rests," Mr. Emerson said. The judge looked a little surprised. He expected a whole parade of character witnesses. He pulled his watch from his pocket and looked at the time.

"I'm going to call a recess until tomorrow morning at nine o'clock. The prosecution and defense will each give their closing arguments at that time. Court is now adjourned." He banged his gavel and retreated to his chambers. As the people began filing out of the courtroom, Ethan turned around to look at Travis for the first time. They made eye contact and held each other's gaze for only a few seconds, but it was all that Ethan needed to know that Travis still loved him. The deputy grabbed Ethan by the arm and hauled him back to the jailhouse.

Chapter Seven

After Travis took his mother home, he came back into town and paid Mr. Emerson another visit. Willie was already seated in a well-crafted, polished wood chair. Mr. Emerson sat behind his wide oak desk and invited Travis to sit in the remaining chair. His office was cluttered with papers and several volumes of law books lay open. One wall had a large bookcase groaning under a mess of fat-spined books. His filing cabinet hung open, and hanging on the wall was his framed degree from Harvard. Mr. Emerson, his collar open, bowtie undone, and oiled hair disheveled, wrung his hands and hung his head. Travis could tell that he was troubled.

"Gentlemen, I have to be completely honest with you. Things are not going as well as I had hoped. I was prepared for the fact that the judge might allow the testimony concerning the sodomy, but what I didn't expect was that Mr. Dreyer would have found out about your arrest record." He was looking at Willie when he spoke the last line. "I'm afraid I may have underestimated the insight of the prosecutor. Putting you on the stand may have been an error on my part."

"Well then how are you gonna fix it?" Willie asked, shifting in his chair. "We paid you good money to win this case."

"It's not over yet. I still have my closing arguments. Many a jury has been swayed by a really good closing argument. I intend to spend most of the night going over my speech to make sure it's as strong as it can be tomorrow."

They spent nearly two hours talking to Mr. Emerson. He tried to reassure them that there was still a chance of winning, but he also let them know that for all practical purposes they should prepare themselves for the fact that they could very well lose. Just as they were getting up to leave, Mr. Emerson spoke directly to Travis.

"There's one more thing I'd like to say. If we win this case, you need to take Ethan and go as far away from here as you can. It won't be safe for either of you here. Go somewhere where there aren't many people and please, for your own safety, be very, very careful."

Travis understood that Mr. Emerson was trying to be helpful. He looked at Willie to see if Mr. Emerson's words had evoked a reaction. They hadn't. Willie either didn't understand or didn't care. It was dusk when they stepped out onto the street. They parted feeling depressed.

Instead of going home, Travis stopped into the nearest saloon. He had a strong desire for something to dull his senses. He sat down on a barstool looking ever so glum when the curly-haired, handsome, Irish bartender sidled over to him.

"My God, man. You look like you've just lost your best friend."

"You don't know how much I fear that could happen." Travis kept his head hung low and his eyes on the bar.

"What'll it be, partner?"

"I really don't care, just so long as it's really strong. And make it a double." Travis tried to think of the last time he had drunk strong liquor. Over a year at least.

"This'll make you feel better." The bartender set two shot glasses in front of him and filled them both to the rim, splashing little drops onto the bar. He could tell that this was a customer who wanted to drink alone, so he left Travis and went to the other side of the bar to clean glasses.

Travis knocked back the first glass. While he was waiting for it to take effect, he struggled with his thoughts. That nightmare in which Miss Peet branded Ethan was all the more powerful now. Now that she had stood there in court making real accusations, the dream almost felt prophetic. Yet Travis was haunted by the hiss in her voice because he believed her accusation might be true. If he hadn't gone after Ethan none of this would have happened. Ethan would still be working in the general store and reading his books. Maybe his own desires had cost the poor kid his life.

*   *   *

Willie went from Mr. Emerson's office to the jailhouse. The sheriff was on duty, and Willie asked him if he could speak to his brother alone. The lamp had been lit, so that shadows of the bars were cast on Ethan's body. Willie sat down on a little stool in front of Ethan's cell, next to Ethan's dinner tray. He had barely touched the meal – some steak and potatoes.

"Not hungry?" Willie asked. Ethan shook his head.

"I've been talking to your lawyer. He says he can still win this thing. He's preparing a hell of a speech for tomorrow that's gonna get you off."

Willie may not have had the heart to tell Ethan how grim things looked, but Ethan saw it in his eyes.

"Willie, I'm afraid the jury might not care if I'm innocent."

"It's all because of that bitch!" Willie erupted into anger. "I swear Ethan, if anything bad happens to you, I'll kill her! I'll get a rope and hang her in her own schoolroom."

"Willie, no! Then they'll just hang you and Ma won't have anybody. If I die, you have to be there for her."

Willie hung his head. Ethan thought he looked close to tears.

"Ethan, Ma doesn't need me. She needs you. You're the one she's proud of. Dad was proud of me, but Ma thinks I'm no good. If you hang, she'll never get over it. You mean too much to her."

"She still loves you though, even though she's not proud of you. You say Dad was proud of you, but I think he hated me."

"Why do you say that?"

"Because he was ashamed of me. He wanted me to be more like you."

*   *   *

Having finished his second shot glass, Travis could face his

198

memories. He thought back to the first day he laid eyes on Ethan Keller. There was something in those eyes that spoke to an affinity between them. It promised something almost lustful. Not just physical lust, but a lust for adventure. It asked Travis to take him away and share the adventure. And there was something innocent, too, in those eyes that sparked something inside of Travis. But how? How is it possible to tell all that from one look at a perfect stranger? The feeling was genuine. He felt the kindred spirit in Ethan before either of them even knew what it meant for their lives, and the only words Travis had to explain that connection was that Ethan's spirit reached out to his.

He thought of the day he had first taken Ethan out riding on Cleo. When Ethan sat behind him on the horse with his hands gently clutching Travis's waist, it gave him such a giddy feeling he could barely keep from laughing out loud. Just to have Ethan that near him for the first time and to feel his touch – his skin had prickled in anticipation. When Ethan had finished riding Cleo by himself, and trotted up to the spot where Travis was waiting for him, he glowed. He was laughing and seemed so full of life, like a caged animal that had just run free. That was the moment he fell in love.

He shifted his thoughts to the cattle drive and the time he bathed in the river under Ethan's gaze. He had felt so flattered that Ethan was curious about his body, and wished he had not scared Ethan off by returning the gaze – but at that point he trusted it was only a matter of time before they were united.

*   *   *

"Do you think Ma will ever tell us what really happened with Dad?" Ethan asked.

"You mean who killed Dad and why?" Willie said. "What makes you think she knows?"

"I just have this feeling that she does."

"Well you know Ma. When it comes to stuff like that, wild horses couldn't drag it out of her. If we ever find out, it won't be from her."

Ethan had lain down on the bed looking out the window at the stars. Willie couldn't see his tears.

"How much time do they give you after you're sentenced to

hang?"

"I don't know, little brother. I'm sure they don't hang you right away. Don't be thinkin' on such things."

"Do you think Ma will come and say goodbye before? I mean if I do get…"

"Ethan, stop. I can't talk about these things. It hurts too much. I don't want you to die. You're my only brother and brothers look out for one another."

It was his awkward way of telling Ethan that he loved him, and he stayed as long as he could. They spent half an hour in silence, Ethan lying on the bed, Willie sitting on the stool with his back against the wall. The Sheriff came in and told them visiting time was over, and turned out the lamp and escorted Willie out.

*   *   *

It was during the rains when Ethan came into his tent wet and shivering. Stripping Ethan out of his clothes and then stripping out of his own was so natural he hadn't hesitated. The warmth radiated between their naked bodies. And how could he think of that night without also considering their night together in the hotel after Josh died? Ethan became *his* protector that night. He had never even considered the possibility that Ethan might actually take care of him and offer him comfort and strength. Travis closed his eyes and conjured up the memory of the two of them in that hotel bed, Ethan spooning his back.

"Hello cowboy, are you looking for some company?" Travis looked up to see a skinny blonde woman with large breasts in a low-cut, tight dress and an overabundance of makeup. "You look like you need a good time, honey."

"Go to hell!" Travis slurred. The woman recoiled, but she was used to surliness with drinking men. She shrugged and walked away, in search of another potential client. The Irishman eased back to Travis's end of the bar.

"Sir, I realize she may be no lady, but you've no cause to speak to a woman like that. I'll ask that you pay for your drinks and be on your way."

Travis scowled, tossed a few coins on the bar and left. Around eighty-thirty, the sun had set, and the Cain homestead was nearly enveloped in darkness; only a faint glow remained on the western horizon. He put Cleo in her stall and fed her some oats, but was too tired to brush her out. The last of the liquor's anesthesia was wearing off and he was in a very dark mood when he entered the house. His mother sat alone with the lamps turned down to the strength of a candle. She had been waiting for him and he could see her mood was as black as his own.

"I've sent the girls to bed early, Travis," she said. "What did you find out from the lawyer?"

"It's not looking good." Travis rested his arm on the mantel. He was not facing her because he wanted to keep his pain private.

"I was hoping the lawyer would find a way to win this. I think I might possibly need to testify."

"What are you talking about?" A single ray of light had broken through the gloom of his mind and he turned to face her.

"I have some information, Travis."

"By all means, Mother, what is it?"

"After you and your father fought that morning, he was in a blind rage all day long. He kept saying to me that if he ever laid eyes on that Ethan Keller again, he would kill him. I didn't believe he would really try to do it. I thought he would cool off and everything would go back to normal."

"Mother, we must go and see Mr. Emerson right now! You must tell him this. Do you know what this means? He can put you on the stand and you can prove Ethan's story! You can save him!"

"I know. But before I agree to do it Travis, I need to know one thing."

"What?"

She paused a moment and swallowed hard. He could tell it was a difficult question for her.

"Is it true the things they have been saying about you and Ethan? I need to know."

"Of course it's not true! How could you even think it?"

"But then why did that schoolteacher say the things she did?"

"I don't know, mother. I have an idea though. Before the cattle drive, when I first met Ethan, she was very interested in me. She was trying to spark an interest in me to get me to start courting her. But I wanted none of it and I think this may be her way of getting back at me."

She let loose a dry, mirthless chuckle. "Hell hath no fury like a woman scorned."

"Something like that."

"Go hitch up the horses, Travis, and I'll get my coat.

*   *   *

The court was assembled and waiting at nine o'clock sharp. The only difference was that spectators flooded the courtroom. They filled the seats and packed themselves into the room along the walls. They bewildered Ethan and even seemed to upset Mr. Emerson. They glared and craned their necks. As the judge took his seat, there was a buzz of gossiping voices. He banged his gavel several times and ordered quiet in the courtroom. Travis, Mrs. Cain and Willie sat in the front row with unflinching countenances.

"Court is now in session. We are ready for your closing arguments, Mr. Dreyer."

"Your Honor?" Mr. Emerson interrupted. "Some new evidence was just presented to me last night, and if I might beg the court's indulgence, I would like to call another witness."

Mr. Dreyer's head jerked over in surprise and he looked most put out. This was obviously going to affect the closing arguments he had already prepared.

"Okay Mr. Emerson, you may call your witness."

"I would like to call to the stand Mrs. Benjamin Cain."

A collective gasp erupted from the crowd and their buzz grew louder. The idea of the wife to defend the murderer of her husband was just scandalous. The Judge banged his gavel, shouting, "Order! Order!"

With her head held high, Mrs. Cain made her way to the witness chair. She wore the same black dress she had worn yesterday, but she had relinquished the veil. Her red hair was demurely pulled back into a knot. She raised her right hand and placed her left on the Bible.

"Do you swear to tell the truth, the whole truth, and nothing but the truth, so help you God?"

"I do." She took the stand.

"Please state your full name for the court."

"Catherine Marie Cain."

"You are the widow of the victim, Mr. Benjamin Cain?"

"I am."

"Mrs. Cain, could you please tell the court what happened on the day your husband was killed?"

"That morning, after my three daughters had gone to school, my son Travis came to the house. Right away Travis and my husband got into a fight. My husband was accusing him of being a... sodomite, and screamed at him that he was bringing shame and disgrace to the whole family. My husband had a very hot temper and he was so angry he began punching Travis in the face. Travis didn't hit his father back, instead he tried to hold him back but was unable to. Finally Travis escaped from his father's blows and left the property. All that day my husband was in a rage. He stormed around the house and kept saying that Ethan Keller was the cause of all this and if he ever laid eyes on him again, he would kill him. At the time I didn't really believe he would do it. I just thought he was blowing off steam, and after a good night's sleep he would forget all about it.

"Later that night, I believe it was around nine o'clock, my husband had been looking out the window. He must have saw something because he went outside. I just thought it must be coyotes. Anyway I heard some banging about out there and I went out to see what was happening and that's when I found him in the barn with Ethan. I believe you know the rest.

"And my son is *not* a sodomite. Those are just vicious rumors started by that awful schoolteacher, Miss Peet!"

"Your Honor, I object!" Mr. Dreyer said. "She's speculating! She doesn't know who started the rumors."

"Mrs. Cain, please just stick with your story and do not make comments about other testimony. The jury will disregard the witness's last statement."

"Mrs. Cain," Mr. Emerson continued, "could you tell us what you found in the barn?"

"Certainly. I found the axe."

Everybody in the courtroom perked up, especially Mr. Dreyer.

"And just where was the axe?"

"It was in the hay by the horse stalls. Which was exactly where it must have landed when…"

"Speculation, Your Honor!" interrupted Mr. Dreyer.

"Mrs. Cain, just answer the questions. Don't offer any opinions."

"I'm sorry, Your Honor."

"Thank you Mrs. Cain. I have no further questions."

"Mr. Dreyer, would you care to cross-examine?"

"Oh yes, Your Honor." Mr. Dreyer leaped up from his chair and dashed across the floor to face the witness personally. "Mrs. Cain, why have you come forward at the last minute to testify? Who put you up to it? Was it perhaps your son? Did your son ask you to testify?"

"Well, yes, but only after I had told him the truth."

"When did you find the axe, Mrs. Cain?"

"Just last night."

"Mrs. Cain, does your son have access to the barn?"

"Yes, of course, he keeps his horse in the barn."

"And what, may I ask, gave you the idea to look for the axe? Did someone suggest that you look for it? Did perhaps your son tell you to look for the axe?" He squinched up his face and said in a mock voice, *"Hey mother, why don't you see if you can find the axe in the barn?* I withdraw the question, Your Honor. No further questions." After this rapid-fire tirade Mr. Dreyer sat down, quite pleased with himself.

"Your Honor, I've been asked a question and I would like to answer it," Mrs. Cain said.

"I'm sorry Mrs. Cain but the question has been withdrawn. You cannot answer."

"Your honor, may I redirect?" Mr. Emerson asked.

"You may."

"Mrs. Cain, why did you look for the axe?"

Mr. Dreyer sulked.

"Thank you, Mr. Emerson. I knew the axe had been missing from the woodshed ever since the night my husband was killed. I naturally assumed that the sheriff had taken it as evidence. Yesterday when I heard that the sheriff did not have the axe and hadn't found it, I took it upon myself to look for it when I got home. My son had no part in it. He didn't even know that I found it."

"Thank you, Mrs. Cain. No further questions."

"You may step down, ma'am. Does the defense rest, *again*?" asked the judge.

"Yes, Your Honor."

"Mr. Dreyer, you may now start your closing arguments."

Mr. Dreyer stood up and placed himself directly in front of the jury box to face the jurors.

"Gentleman of the jury, you have heard the testimony and have seen the evidence. It is now up to you to weigh what you have seen and heard and to mete out justice. It was shown in the trial that this man..." he pointed at Ethan, "did kill Mr. Benjamin Cain. He was found crouching over the body with the murder weapon by his side. Oh yes, he *claimed* he was acting in self-defense and that the victim was trying to kill him with an axe. But this is a fact – the sheriff thoroughly searched the barn and no axe was found. There was some late testimony you just heard this morning about the axe being discovered in a haystack. But I say that it is possible, even probable, that the axe was planted there to exonerate the defendant. I just ask that you carefully consider the *source* of that testimony.

"I also ask that you consider the character of the defendant. His own schoolteacher has testified that he confessed to her that he was in *love* with the son of the victim. Draw whatever conclusions from that that you will. You have heard testimony that the victim had knowledge of sodomy accusations against Mr. Keller. I say that the defendant saw Mr. Benjamin Cain as a threat that would prevent him from obtaining what he desired and thereby had motive to murder him. It is likely that he hid out in the barn, waited for Mr. Cain to come out and took him by surprise, bashing his head with a shovel. This man must pay for the life he took. Convict him. See that justice is served." Mr. Dreyer quietly sat down. The whole courtroom sat in silence pondering his argument.

"Mr. Emerson, your closing arguments, please."

Mr. Emerson also got up and faced the jury, but he walked

back and forth in front of the jury box, making eye contact with every juror before he spoke.

"Gentleman, you have before you a very important task. A man's life hangs in the balance of what you decide today. We all know that when a man commits a crime and is tried and convicted and pays for that crime, justice is served and that is good. But sometimes, and this is one of those times, the justice system gets too enthusiastic and an innocent man gets caught in the web. Under our system of law, it is the duty of the prosecution to prove to you beyond a doubt that a man is guilty. And should the prosecution fail to remove all doubt as they have in this case, it is *your* duty to find him not guilty. Should you find him guilty and have a doubt of his guilt, then that is something you will carry on your conscience for the rest of your days.

"Let's examine the evidence in this case. First of all we are in agreement that Mr. Keller killed Mr. Cain. That is not in question. However, he did not *murder* him. The first bit of evidence is that he did not flee the scene. He stayed and waited for the sheriff to come and question him. This is not the behavior of a guilty man. The prosecution was unable to give you any reasonable explanation for this. The sheriff admitted that he had never arrested a man who had committed murder that did not flee the scene.

"Next there are the accusations of Miss Peet. Whether or not you believe that the defendant is a sodomite is irrelevant to this case. It simply has no bearing. However let me point out that not one shred of evidence was given to prove that he *is* a sodomite. It was only said that he declared love for another man which is not a crime if you choose to believe that testimony at all. But where the sodomy rumors are relevant is with the victim. You have heard testimony from the wife of the victim that he believed the rumors about Mr. Keller and his son and in my book that gives the victim motive to kill. From his own wife's testimony, he threatened to kill Mr. Keller. And you've heard testimony that the missing axe was in the barn all the time, concealed in the hay. It was through the sheriff's negligence that it was not discovered in the first place. Now Mr. Dreyer in his closing arguments asked you to disregard the testimony given by Mrs. Cain and yet he contradicts himself by saying testimony was given that the victim had knowledge of the sodomy rumors. Yes, he was referring to Mrs. Cain's testimony and asking you to accept that part of it! Ethan Keller acted in self-defense. Even if you are not positive of this, you are also not positive of his guilt, and wherever there is doubt, you must not convict."

Mr. Emerson sat down and once again the crowd was pensive.

"The jury will now retire for debate." the judge said. The bailiff led the jury out through the judge's chambers to a hall a block away. The spectators all went outside to get some fresh air while they waited for the jury to come back. Ethan and the lawyers remained in their seats to wait. Deputy Amos stood guard over him. The judge disappeared into his chambers. The only spectators that had remained inside were Travis, Willie and Mrs. Cain. Ethan now turned to look at Travis. They looked into each others eyes but they were both so petrified with fear that they felt nothing.

Forty-five minutes later the jury returned to the courtroom. Ethan watched them nervously. None of them would even look in his direction. The spectators all poured back in, eager for the first-rate entertainment of a verdict. The judge came back in. Ethan was clenching his fists so tight his knuckles were white.

"Has the jury reached a verdict?" the judge asked.

"We have, Your Honor," said the foreman, one of the neatly dressed businessmen.

"What say you?"

"In the case against Ethan Keller on the charge of murder in the first degree, we find the defendant...guilty."

The courtroom erupted with cheers and applause. Ethan felt his heart stop. He turned pale and began to tremble. Travis's mouth fell open and he felt dizzy like he was about to faint. Mrs. Cain dabbed her eyes with a handkerchief and Willie glared at the jurors. All the commotion turned into one big blur for Ethan. He was simply in Hell.

The judge banged his gavel on the desk for a full minute. Finally the cheers died down and became whispers, and the judge spoke.

"I am going to call a recess for two hours. I am not prepared to pass sentence and I need some time to think. Court will resume in two hours."

The deputy grabbed Ethan and hauled him back to the jailhouse. As he was being led away, different faces scowled at him. He was now a convicted felon and they let him know it.

*   *   *

That afternoon court reconvened with the same vicious crowd as before. Ethan sat at the defense table, feeling nothing. The judge had taken a little while longer than two hours. The crowd was restless. They wanted blood. Travis could hear stray conversions about the excitement of a public execution. It infuriated him, but he buried the emotions and kept a straight face hoping that Ethan was not able to hear the terrible things people were saying. Travis rubbed his sweating palms on his pant legs; he was on the verge of hyperventilating. Finally the Judge came in and took his seat. He looked troubled.

"This case has been a hard one for me. I've given it a lot of thought and I've wrestled with the decision I have been forced to make. First let me say that the jury has chosen to convict, and had I been on that jury, I'm not certain I would have been in agreement with them. Nevertheless, it is the verdict and as such it will stand. Before I pass sentence I would like to give a word of warning. In this case there was no proof that any act of sodomy was committed. I admonish the sheriff and the prosecutor *not* to attempt to press sodomy charges against either of these boys. Now due to certain circumstances, I have chosen not to impose the maximum sentence in this case…"

Boos began emanating from the crowd. The judge banged his gavel to restore order.

"Ethan Keller, would you please rise."

Ethan and his lawyer stood up.

"In the case against you, you have been found guilty of murder in the first degree by a jury of your peers. I hereby sentence you to five years in prison with hard labor. Court is now adjourned."

The crowd became unruly with booing and shouts of

injustice. Travis threw back his head and closed his eyes. A wave of relief rushed over him.

Ethan's knees buckled and he put his hands on the table to steady himself. Had he heard right? He wasn't going to hang? Through the throng of people Ethan looked for Travis. He saw him. Travis and his mother were holding each other in a tight embrace. Suddenly Ethan felt someone grab his arm. It was the deputy, and he began dragging Ethan away.

"TRAVIS!" Ethan reached toward him. Travis released his mother and looked at Ethan. There was nothing he could do but watch.

The courtroom grew hotter. The buzz of voices droned in the air. The deputy's stout fingers gripped Ethan's slender bicep, bunching up his shirt. The show was over, and the jurors began to rise and file out of the box. A fat juror wearing a vest blocked half of Ethan; two more jurors crossed the floor and blocked all but the top of his head. The door next to the judge's chambers opened and all Travis saw was the deputy's hat disappearing before the door closed again.

Epilogue

October 1883. The mid-morning Texas sun beat down upon a thirty foot prison wall. Directly facing the ten foot high double doors, a small brown wagon harnessed to a black gelding was parked under an oak tree about fifty yards away, the only shade in the midst of a dry dusty landscape. Sitting in the driver's seat was a smartly dressed man. He had been patiently waiting there all morning. There was a clang as the doors were unbolted and slowly opened up. The sentry who had pulled open the door stepped aside and a man trudged through the doorway. The doors clanged shut behind him. He was dressed in drab prison garb and carried his few belongings in a bag slung over his shoulder. He looked around like he wasn't sure where he was to go or what he had to do. The man in the wagon snapped the whip once and drove up to the doors, turning to the left just before reaching them so that the right side of the wagon now faced the newly released inmate. He held out his hand to the man on the ground.

"Ethan."

"Travis!" His white teeth accented his rough brown face. "I didn't know whether or not you were going to be here. My God, you look exactly the same as the last time I saw you." He took Travis's hand, stepped up into the wagon, and sat down beside him on the buckboard.

"Of course I'm here. I've been waiting a long time for this

day."

Although Travis's appearance was the same, Ethan's was quite altered. Five years of hard labor had given him the muscular body of a real man. Every ounce of adolescence had been hammered, lifted, driven, and beaten from his body. The alabaster skin of his neck was rugged and weathered. Prison life had aged him beyond his twenty-two years; to look at the two men now, no one would know there was any difference in age between them. As they pulled away from the prison, Travis gazed upon Ethan's face, taking in every feature. He couldn't get over how different he looked. The soft brown eyes were the same, but he no longer had the face of a boy. It was a rough, masculine face, and to Travis's eyes, Ethan was more handsome than ever.

"Where are we going?" Ethan asked.

"To the nearest town. I've got a hotel room there so we can get you cleaned up and out of those prison clothes."

Ethan nodded. They rode along for some time in silence. To Ethan, the five years of separation had made them feel awkward, almost like they were strangers again. But to Travis Ethan seemed much more withdrawn, like a horse whose spirit had been broken. Every once in a while, he would put his arm around Ethan and give him an affectionate little squeeze, sort of a half-hug. After a long silence, Ethan said, "How come you never came to visit me in prison?"

The question stung Travis's heart. He knew it was coming, and he felt ashamed, knowing that it was the one way he had failed Ethan. But the truth was he had let his fear win over doing what he knew was right.

"Ethan, you'll never know how desperately I wanted to come. It tore me up inside to stay away, but I just couldn't take the chance. I'm so, so sorry. You probably thought that I had abandoned you."

"I wondered if maybe you had." After another stretch of silence, he said, "My mother came to see me twice. She was very sad and didn't have much to say to me."

"I'm sorry, Ethan. I'm sure your mother loves you, she's just not a very strong woman."

"I know. And Willie came to see me eight times. I kept count."

"You've got a good brother, there. Despite his faults, he always stood by you. Now I wish I had gotten in contact with him so I could have sent you a message."

"So where are you taking me? After we go to the hotel, I mean."

A smile broke across Travis's lips. "Now Ethan, that's a secret. You're just going to have to wait to find out when we get there."

"Why? Aren't you going to take me back home to my mother?"

"No."

"So you're really not going to tell me where we're going?"

"Nope. You're just going to have to trust me, Ethan."

Ethan accepted this. Travis wondered at his docility. Had prison merely broken his spirit, or did Ethan still have complete faith in him?

*　　*　　*

Right around suppertime, they arrived at the Lone Star Hotel. It was one of the largest buildings Ethan had ever seen, besides prison, painted white and looking stately. Travis dropped off the horse and wagon at the stable and he and Ethan went inside to check in. The lobby had polished marble floors, original oil paintings of Texas landmarks and elegant statues of Davy Crockett and Sam Houston in the corners. After Travis checked in they ascended the grand staircase, followed by the bellman carrying Travis's large trunk. When they entered their room, Ethan's eyes widened. The room was decorated with flowery wallpaper and heavy, fine draperies. There were two beds, a divan, a writing desk, a vanity, and a large bathtub. After five years in a prison cell with a lumpy little bed, this seemed like heaven. Travis asked the bellman if he could see to it that the bathtub was filled with warm water. While several maids went back and forth bringing pails of warm water and pouring them into the bathtub, Travis opened the trunk and began laying clothes out on the bed. There were brand new shirts and trousers, undergarments, boots and a coat.

"Some of these might be a little tight on you. You've grown some."

"This is all for me?"

"Of course."

Just as the maids had finished filling the tub, room service arrived. The bellman wheeled in a cart containing an entire meal for two all hidden under shiny round lids, accepted his tip, and bowed from the doorway. Travis locked the door behind him. He drew the window shades and lit the lamps with the wicks turned down low. They pulled up chairs to each end of the cart, which was large enough to serve as a table, and removed the lids. Chicken with cream sauce, boiled green beans and carrots, fresh-baked bread and tapioca pudding – the aroma was hypnotizing. As they ate, they watched each other's faces, re-memorizing the lips, the curve of their brows, the way their skin moved when they smiled. Ethan had spent the past five years envisioning Travis's face and body. Now he was seeing that face again for real and he knew that soon he would be seeing Travis's body again. Ethan had been celibate for five years. Not that he had any choice, but if he had, he would have chosen to wait for Travis. He couldn't contain the joy he felt and a big smile spread across his lips. Travis was so pleased to see that smile that he laughed out loud.

"That's the kid I remember," he said.

When they finished eating, Travis said, "Come on, let's take a bath before the water gets cold." Ethan didn't know why, but he suddenly felt shy. He watched Travis undress and step into the bathtub. Then he got so excited, he couldn't get his clothes off fast enough and almost fell over trying to get his pants off. When Ethan finally stood before him completely naked, Travis had to smile, for Ethan's manhood stood out before him like a flagpole. Travis lay back in the bathtub and Ethan climbed in on top of him. They had their first kiss in five years and it was a kiss worth waiting for. Ethan rose up off of Travis. Travis reached up and caressed his biceps and tight chest muscles.

"My, oh my, how you've developed," Travis said dreamily. "And look at all that hair on your chest! You certainly didn't have that last time I saw you."

Ethan smiled, but discussion about his body embarrassed him. He was still modest. Once they finished bathing they went to bed, and spent half the night renewing their love until they had spent themselves. As Ethan lay in Travis arms, he finally felt safe again. In prison, he had held out hope that maybe he and Travis would be reunited, but he had prepared himself for the possibility that Travis, or for that matter love, was lost to him forever. Now those fears were vanquished and he was where he belonged.

*   *   *

The next morning they set off toward Travis's secret destination. The passion of the night before had broken the awkwardness and Ethan came out of his shell. Their conversations covered a wide range of topics – from books Ethan had remembered reading to the state of affairs in the country. The one thing they didn't talk about was their route. Ethan was burning up with curiosity. He didn't want to try and wheedle it out of him, because Travis wanted to surprise him and he respected that, and people who wheedle secrets now gave him a sour taste.

"Travis, I know you're not going to tell me where we're going, but could you at least tell me how long it's going to take to get there?"

"Now *that* I'll tell you. It should take us about two and a half weeks, maybe less if the weather's good."

That gave Ethan a good idea. They were definitely leaving Texas. And based on the fact that they were traveling northwest, Ethan guessed that maybe they were going to Colorado. He couldn't be sure because he hadn't traveled enough to judge travel times and distances. But that answer satisfied him and he prepared himself for the two-week journey, knowing he would travel to the ends of the earth if need be just so long as he was with Travis.

The days went by and the weather held. They made good time on the trail. At night they would camp. In the wagon Travis carried a tent, which they would pitch as soon as the sun went down. He also carried an ample supply of food, mostly canned goods and some dried meats. They would cook supper by the fire and lay out under the stars until they got sleepy and crawled into their tent to snuggle up in their bedroll. At first they fell into the familiar habit of suppressing physical contact outside the tent, but then soon realized that there were no other human beings around for miles. They were just so happy to be in one another's company that they were not bored by the routine and the two weeks went by rather quickly.

There was only one discomfort that nagged at Ethan's mind. Whenever Ethan brought up the subject of what Travis had been doing for the past five years, Travis evaded him. All he'd say was, "Nothing much, just working a little here and there," and then change the subject. It made Ethan suspicious that maybe during his absence, Travis had found someone else. It gnawed at his mind but he couldn't bring himself to ask the question. He feared the answer, but didn't suppose he could hold it against him if he had been with another man. But the thought of him pining away in prison while Travis was out having intimate relations with another man would be a sharp bone to digest. He tried to think of other things and stopped prying into Travis's affairs.

Six days shy of the two and a half weeks, they were traveling in some rough country and went over such a large hole that they broke an axle. Travis hopped down from the cart and knelt in the dirt.

"Damn! We had less than a week to go." He pitched his hat against the cart. "Now what the hell are we going to do?"

"Can't you fix it?" Ethan asked.

"There's not a wheelwright within a hundred miles of here. This axle is broken clean in two. There's no way to bind it back together. We have to find another axle somehow."

"Couldn't we just leave the wagon and ride the horse to wherever we're going?" Ethan was just trying to be helpful, but Travis was all out of sorts.

"I didn't even bring a saddle. You know how uncomfortable it is to ride bareback for that long, Ethan?"

Travis mopped his brow and picked up his hat. He plied its brim, lost in thought. Meanwhile Ethan poked his head under the back of the wagon to study the broken axle. It was split cleanly in two with one half pointing at the ground and the other half sticking up touching the wagon bed. After about twenty minutes, Ethan sat down next to Travis.

"Travis, you got plenty of rope?"

"Sure, why?"

Ethan's face lit up. "I've got an idea. You just have that rope ready and I'll be back." Ethan ran off into the direction of some bushes. Travis was puzzled but he pulled the rope out of the back of the wagon and sat down on the wagon bed to wait for Ethan.

Forty-five minutes later Ethan came walking back with a bundle of branches in his arms. They were all neatly broken into three to four foot lengths.

"You don't mean to tell me you're going to make an axle out of those!" Travis said.

"Not exactly. Can I use your knife?"

Travis handed it to him. He began whittling all the twigs and bumps off the branches until they were as smooth as he could make them. Ethan got under the wagon, took five of the branches and held them all around the broken axle.

"Now bring that rope under here and start tying these together," Ethan instructed.

"Ah... now I understand. You're making a splint to hold the axle together."

"That's right. But the ropes have to be wrapped around and tied really tight or it won't work."

Travis was clever with knots, and he bound up the branches so they were as good as welded. When they were all in place, Travis drove the wagon and Ethan watched the wheels. The axle was just a little wobbly, but they could probably make it to Denver for a new axle. Ethan climbed back up on the buckboard and they got on the road again.

"Sometimes you really surprise me," said Travis, shaking his head and smiling, "Just keep an eye on those wheels. If they start to get too loose we'll have to redo the ropes."

The last two days were the roughest. Gullies and rocks and buttes obstructed their way. The wobbly axle didn't help matters when they started climbing through the mountain passes. The landscape was lush and the mountain air fresh. They rode into the city of Denver. Nestled beside the giant mountain range, it was a tidy, rustic town. The streets were flat, made of moist dark dirt, and all of the buildings and sidewalks were built of yellow pine. Travis confessed that he had not originally planned to come into Denver, but since they needed a new axle and Denver was so close, they changed course, dropped the wagon off at the wheelwright and got a small room for the night. It was above a saloon and noisy, but they were tired and slept soundly.

The next morning Ethan was wakened by Travis shaking his shoulder. He yawned and rubbed his eyes; Travis was already dressed.

"Rise and shine; we need to make an early start."

"Why?" Ethan said, through a yawn.

"Because we only got seventy miles to go and I want to get there before sundown, the day after tomorrow. What I want to show you needs to be seen in daylight."

Ethan perked up. He cleared his head, splashed some water on his face and got dressed. Travis had already got the wagon back from the wheelwright, and paid the hotel bill, and as soon as Ethan came outside they hopped in the wagon and were off.

"Aren't we even going to eat breakfast?" Ethan asked. Travis reached in his shirt pocket and pulled out a strip of jerky.

As they left the bustle of Denver behind them, it instantly came clear why the final seventy miles was going to take three days. They were headed straight into the heart of the Rocky Mountains. By noon they had reached the foothills and the ascent grew steeper and rougher. They were entering into terrain that hadn't been broken in with roads or trails. Some of the hills and gullies required both men to get out and push the wagon; their splinted axle would never have survived this country. As the sun reached its zenith and began its slow decent into the west, they were up high enough that, looking back, they saw Denver's angular layout of buildings and streets. From this elevation it looked like a toy village. No sooner had they resumed their course when they arrived at a new wonder – there in front of him, on the mountainside, stood the most beautiful, monolithic rock formations Ethan had ever seen. The red sandstone was made up of crystalline layers that had slowly been pushed up from the earth's crust. As they passed by each great sculpture, Ethan craned his neck, gaping in wonder. Travis grinned the whole way, and he stopped the wagon when they came to the largest rock monuments yet. On the gentle incline before them stood two mammoth, precipitous slabs, each three hundred feet high, and each nearly symmetrical.

Ethan finally found his voice. "What is this place?"

"I've heard it's been called The Garden of Angels," Travis said. "But most people just call it Red Rocks."

Ethan hopped down and turned in a slow circle. "You know," he said, "it's almost like a great coliseum."

"And we are standing in the arena."

After they spent nearly a half an hour sitting, entranced by the sacredness of that place, Travis snapped the reins.

*   *   *

The next two days they climbed mountain passes, crossed streams, and slipped between forest groves until at last, late in the afternoon on the third day, they came to one final hill.

As they came up over the crest of that hill, Travis turned to Ethan and said, "We're home."

Laid out in front of him was the exact dream ranch that Travis had described to Ethan over five years ago: the brown house, the porch that wrapped all around, the hill with the mountains behind it and the river valley below. Trees punctuated the landscape and the entire property was surrounded by wooden fences. About twenty yards from the house was a barn and several horses grazed in the fields.

"You built all of this?" Ethan said in amazement.

"I built it for you. For us."

"So that's what you've been doing for the last five years," Ethan said in awe as he took it all in. He could hardly believe it was all real.

Travis watched Ethan's expression as he drove toward the ranch house. He took great pleasure in Ethan's astonishment. He pulled the wagon up to the front of the house and jumped down. A young curly-haired man stepped out onto the porch.

"Hello, Señor Travis, you are back!"

"Ethan, this is Guillermo. He's our ranch hand. He's been taking care of the horses while I've been away."

"Nice to meet you, Señor Ethan. I've heard a lot about you."
He reached out and shook Ethan's hand.

"Come on inside, Ethan. I want to show you around." Travis
led him into the house. It was neat and clean and the fresh-cut-
timbers made it look and smell brand-new. The living room was
simply furnished with a bear-skin rug and a couple of rocking
chairs. The kitchen had simple wooden shelves containing a
short stack of dishes, a little collection of mugs, a modest column
of bowls. There was a pot-belly stove and a wash basin and a
square table with four chairs for dining. A trap-door in the
kitchen floor led to a cellar that was well stocked with grain,
tubers, and canned goods. There were three bedrooms, one for
storage, one for Guillermo, and the third had a large bed and a
bureau. There was no glass in any of the windows, and there was
no need for curtains. The windows simply had wooden shutters
that could be locked up tight at night.

"So what do you think Ethan? Do you like it?"

"I love it. It's perfect."

Travis gripped the bedpost with his hand and looked down at
the floor. Clearly he needed to say something, but he struggled to
find the words. "When you first went to prison, I thought I was
going to go crazy. I didn't know how I was going to get through
five long years waiting for you. The only way I could survive
was to do something. So I built this ranch out of my love for
you. This ranch is built on our love. I poured everything that I
am into this place so that I could give it to you."

Ethan reached out and put his hand on top of Travis's, then
moved closer and laid his head on his shoulder. "I almost don't
know what to say except that I love you very, very much."

"Oh! I've got one more thing to show you! Guillermo!"
Travis called, and he pulled Ethan back outside.

"Yes, Señor Travis?"

"Where's Cleo?"

"She's in the barn, Señor."

"Come on." Travis grabbed Ethan by the hand and led him to
the barn.

Ethan was startled. As soon as they were out of earshot
Ethan asked, "Guillermo, is he…?"

"Yes, Ethan. He's one of us. We can be ourselves and be totally honest around him. He's completely trustworthy."

"Did you and he…?"

"*No*, Ethan. Ever since the day I first met you I haven't been with anyone else." Travis slowly pulled open the barn door. Light flooded into the barn; fresh hay was scattered about, and sacks of oats were stacked against the wall. Cleo slowly walked towards them, followed by a beautiful sorrel foal, nudging for its mother's milk.

"There she is, Ethan – A filly, just for you."

Ethan dropped to his knees beside the filly. His eyes flooded with tears. He wrapped his arms around her and gently pulled her to his body. He could feel her warmth and the softness of her hair against his cheek. She was so small and frail; he could feel her ribs and the beating of her tiny heart. The filly squirmed and bucked against him.

"She's going to be a strong one."

The end